A

Dreamed Of

J Edward Neill

Cover Art 'The Jupiter Event' by Amanda Makepeace

Tessera Guild Publishing

Téssera

ISBN-13: 978-1516971831
ISBN-10: 1516971833

We'd reached a state of such automatic bliss, such hedonistic indulgence, that when woken by the noise of war, our first reaction was disbelief. Why would anyone think to end our perfect peace? Who would dream of disturbing utopia? We assumed our enemies were envious of our perfection. We reasoned they wanted us out so they could get In. Everyone would want In, we thought. And why wouldn't they?

But we soon came to our senses. We remembered long ago, before such things as In, emotion, passion, and yearning were a part of humanity. And we remembered the most powerful of all reasons for one human to desire the destruction of another:

Vengeance.

The Jupiter Event

Nine hundred years ago, humanity believed it had attained perfection.

The ugly wars of the Twenty-Second Century had ground to an end. New systems of farming and weather-control had eliminated hunger. Cancer, heart disease, diabetes, even Alzheimer's—cured by a single scientist's genetic research. Coal, oil, and gas, long the mainstays of 'dirty' energy, were eliminated, replaced by nuclear-powered machines which operated like miniature stars, and which were built to last not for hundreds of years, but for *millions*.

It seemed humanity had climbed a mountain for many centuries dreamed of.

And yet, if it were true, if humanity had finally transcended, it had little to do with the decline of poverty, hunger, conflict, and war. For even with all obstacles removed, people still sought to undermine, to steal, to envy, and to seek power when utterly unnecessary.

Ultimately, what brought us so near to utopia was the ultimate weapon for suppressing human instinct and emotion:

Entertainment.

In the year 2116, a technology firm known as pENT (Permanent Entertainment) ended their focus on creating video games. The art had long been in decline. Even with the most immersive games available and with entire city blocks dedicated to round-the-clock gaming experiences, the world's youth craved more. No one needed to work, after all. No soldiers were required to wage war, and no labor force was required. Leisure time had become *all the time*. To exist, the world's youth needed only to rise from sleep, claim a meal at any of a billion free-of-charge food dispensers, and *breathe*. Nothing else was mandatory. All sectors of labor had become fully mechanized, controlled by robotic automatons, who, even when in need of maintenance, were simply repaired by other automatons.

Life had become easy. Too easy.

And so Permanent Entertainment decided to live up to its name.

And in a matter of months, pENT released a beta version of *In*.

In, or Imaginary Nature, was at first meant as a life simulator. Early users would plug in for days, even weeks at a time. While jacked into *In*, users could create every tiny detail of an alternate existence, and then live that existence as though it were their own. Some *In* testers used it to escape their utter boredom. Others, most especially young men, used it to simulate every imaginable sexual adventure. Women created fantastical lands, many of which lacked men, and nearly all of which gave them the chance to be the most beautiful, most fashionable, and most influential person alive. The elderly used *In* to be young again. Artists created other worlds to inhabit, some alien, some mechanical, and many that were terrifying. The earliest beta users became so adept at using *In*'s interface that they created empires over which they ruled and galactic civilizations designed to worship them. Some even used *In* to recreate themselves as gods, suzerains of everyone and everything.

It was all fantasy, of course.

And yet, ten months after *In*'s beta ended, *In* was almost in.

Having anticipated *In*'s success, pENT tried to make certain its release-day preparations were perfect. In cities around the world, their bots prepared vast volumes of server space. Rows upon rows of buildings were dedicated to housing computers capable of processing users' imaginations. Elsewhere, automatons constructed apartments designed solely for users to live in while jacked into *In*. The apartments had tiny rooms. Most were barely big enough to fit a single chair, a few strands of body-sensory jacks, and a feed/waste tube to keep users from needing to un-jack several times every day. 'Sardine houses,' an elder pENT executive named them. 'Fit for sleeping fish.'

Given their preparations, Permanent Entertainment assumed its success. Their webs of wifi satellites and Blacktooth, light-speed data-ejectors blanketed almost every metropolitan area in North America, Western Europe, China, and the unified, Middle-Eastern goliath Iranabia. They prepped thousands of robots to deal with technical problems, retrofit older connections, and to train users to remember to un-jack.

They couldn't have been more ready.

On the sixth of June, 2120, one hundred and thirty-seven pENT executive officers sat in the top room of the tallest tower in North America. Surrounded on all sides by paper-thin membrane video screens and live-feed holo-generators, men and women in black suits held their breaths as a clock ticked down to zero-hour. If *In* worked, they knew Permanent Entertainment would become the most powerful company in the world. But if it didn't, if the system crashed or users died, pENT execs knew their vast investment of money and capital would have been all for nothing, and their careers would be ruined.

Three...two...one.

The crimson digits hanging in the air ticked toward zero.

When the moment arrived, hundreds of thousands of users simultaneously jacked into *In*.

The execs paled. But the system held.

In was in.

If ever pENT had doubted their work, on that night they knew otherwise. Every *In* chair in every sardine house in every city had been bought and filled. Servers lit up with the countless impulses of users' imaginations, but sped along no slower for it, working at less than one percent of total capacity. Body-sensory jacks invented especially for *In* ensured that users' muscles still fired, breather chairs prevented bedsores, while streams of nutrients pumped in via feed tubes, all working as flawlessly as pENT had hoped.

The next morning, whole cities remained quiet.

Fewer than one percent of users had un-jacked overnight.

A week later, more than ninety-seven percent were still plugged in. It was the beginning of something beautiful.

And of something terrible.

Within a few weeks of *In* going online, the debate began. The world's remaining politicians, though long marginalized to a fraction of their previous power, thrummed with conversations about *In*. Was it immoral that so many users had yet to un-jack, that men and women with families had gone missing by the tens of thousands to pursue lives of pleasure and fantasy? Would the system eventually fail, releasing countless users back into reality, their minds forever ruined by an addiction to a world other than the real?

To counter such concerns, some leaders trumpeted, "This is at last the great release we've sought. The prison of our ordinary consciousness is broken. We're all free."

But others called *In* the '*Great Lie*,' and railed against it with vicious determination.

And so the argument raged.

Whatever the debate, and no matter its legitimacy, pENT's sights were set on larger prize than a few hundred thousand people. In the second month after *In*'s takeoff, automaton factories fired up in earnest. The factories turned out breather chairs and body-sensory jacks by the million. In pENT's underground facilities, robots machined and programmed impossibly powerful servers, which were shipped within days to hubs worldwide, connected to nuclear-powered energy sources, and switched on with the intent of never, ever being switched off.

By the time the debate deepened, half the world's politicians had either plugged into *In* themselves or given up the fight against it. Those who opposed jacking in waged their wars of words upon deaf ears, empty rooms, and membrane video screens no one cared to watch.

By the year 2126, nine-hundred million people had permanently hooked into *In*.

By 2142, supported by pENT automatons working shifts that never ended, the number of *In* users reached eight billion.

In was no longer simply a fantasy.

In was everything.

It became reality, and much more than simple entertainment. With their bodies protected in every way, users spent months jacked into *In*, then years, and after a time they stopped un-jacking entirely. Before the last of the pENT execs gave up their real-world lives and entered the system, they uploaded the libraries of every nation into the system, every book, magazine, scientific journal, and archaic text. With advanced streaming methods users were able to consume everything humanity had spoken or written in the last hundred years. Even the least intelligent people swallowed so much knowledge as to become ten times as educated as any human who had ever lived before them. With such knowledge their imaginations grew, their fantasies increased exponentially, and the reasons for un-jacking became nil.

By 2151, ninety-nine percent of humanity was permanently jacked-in. Cities were silent but for the hum of servers and the rare incoming march of automatons. The robots once created to replace human labor became caretakers for oceans of their eternally dreaming masters. The world of the physical fell away into nothing.

The world of the mind had won.

Still, ninety-nine percent was not one-hundred percent, and in the far corners of the sleeping world, millions of humans lived free of *In*. Some had never dared jack-in. Others had jacked-in briefly, but somehow resisted the temptation to fall into forever-long fantasies. These rare sects of society became known derogatorily as *Outs*. The *Ins* were aware of them, though only somewhat, and only through the reports of bots and the occasional un-jacked spy. It didn't matter. In time, the *Ins* came to assume the *Outs* were unimaginative, radical, and in the worst cases, heretical. 'Why would anyone *not* want to be *In*?' they roared within their dreams. 'There's nothing left in the regular world. Not for us. Not for them.'

For many years, the *Outs* existed on the fringes of the sleeping *In* world. They kept all the technologies humanity had mastered, but strove no further. Even when *In* scientists streamed messages back into the physical world, hoping to invite, educate, and beguile, the *Outs* discarded the lessons. The *Ins* with their exponential capacity for learning clawed at the very boundaries of physics, mastering the sciences behind gravity, quantum mechanics, and even time. But the *Outs* wanted no part of it. Their lives had become easy enough without *In*, and with the world so quiet around them, the *Outs* earned such peace and prosperity that no civilization before them had attained.

And none since.

In 2162, the *Outs* gathered in the great city that had once been known as Venice. The Pope and his clergy were gone now, having flocked to the ether in search of God, and the pale streets and dark canals had long gone silent. In a tower high above the sleeping city, the most rebellious of the *Outs* held conclave.

"Unless we put an end to *In*, those who live in fantasy will eventually destroy us," reasoned an *Out* leader. "Whether by misunderstanding, jealousy, or sheer boredom, they'll want us gone."

To his surprise, his remarks were met with cheers.

"They'll want to secure eternity locked away in their minds!" cried one *Out* woman, a politician from the old days.

"Yes," agreed another, "and we're all that's left. If we're gone, no one will ever unplug them. Humanity will die."

"No!" still another shouted. "They've got new machines. Haven't you seen? They breed in their minds. The automatons fertilize their women while their bodies sleep. Their children have never known anything but *In*. Their babies have seen nothing in their lives but the world that *isn't*."

"Grotesque!" screamed a number of *Outs*.

"Disgusting!"

"It must end!"

Even in the darkest corners of their minds, pENT engineers had never foreseen the day when the un-jacked masses would rebel. The world of fantasy had been at first good business, then an unprecedented success, and finally a glorious ascension they assumed all of humanity would embrace. That anyone would ever grow to hate their beautiful creation, they never fathomed.

And such was their mistake.

When a band of *Out* partisans burned an *In* tower to the ground with two-thousand people still jacked-in inside it, the *In* world barely blinked. They had no idea what had really happened. The *Outs* had smashed two dozen guardian automatons and clipped every single body sensory jack in the building. Surviving *Ins* were so consumed by their separate worlds and endless hoarding of knowledge, entertainment, and sex that even when a thousand of their number vanished, they registered almost nothing. They assumed the vanished *Ins* had wandered off to a new fantasy or scientific revelation, and that they'd soon be back.

But three weeks later, when a fringe *Out* group orchestrated the nuclear detonation of an entire sleeping city, the *Ins* caught on. Darkness grew in their hearts. In an imagined place deep within their minds, they gathered to plot their revenge.

Their thoughts turned to violence.

Within hours, they acted.

Without leaving their fantasy worlds, the *Ins* reprogrammed thousands of automatons to return to their factories and retrofit themselves with terrifying new weapons. The advances made by billions of dreaming humans were more than the *Outs* were prepared for. Four days after the nuclear attack, automatons arrived in *Out* cities armed with lasers capable of carving buildings in half, flechette rifles that spewed out thousands of explosive particulates, and gravity-distortion devices that hurled people, vehicles, and houses miles into the air before letting them tumble helplessly back to Earth.

The *Ins'* revenge took the lives of tens of thousands.

Out cities burned.

A war began.

For every city the *Ins'* automatons laid waste to, the *Outs* paid them back in spades. And because of the automaton armies the *Ins* employed to fight their proxy war, the *Outs* forgot such things as mercy. Bombs were laid in the hearts of jacked-in towers, and thousands of dreaming men, women, and children turned to ash. Factories were leveled using explosives, and servers torn apart by the hundreds. For each one life taken by *In* automatons, the *Outs* severed the jacks of scores of *Ins*. In the most pernicious of the *Outs'* attacks, two hundred men cut the servers of some eight-hundred *Ins,* waited outside an apartment for the un-jacked to wander into the streets, and bludgeoned them all to death.

Neither side was righteous.

The *Outs* felt abandoned. The *Ins* felt betrayed.

But before long, the *Ins* gained the upper hand.

The turn of the tide began when an *In* man, Gerrard De Napoli, un-jacked himself in the Old World city of Paris. For twenty years, Gerrard had fashioned imaginary worlds in which war never ended. He knew every tactic of every battle since the medieval days of England's occupation of Scotland,

and had relived them all a hundred times as the general of each side. He was, for lack of an equal, the most accomplished military strategist to ever have lived. It mattered none that he'd never been in a real-world battle. *In* had trained him far better than any soldiering, any amount of eons spent warring in the physical world.

After making himself a stronghold in the heart of Paris, Gerrard quickly established a connection to every pENT server worldwide. He ordered that the greatest minds created by *In* be un-jacked and delivered under automaton escort to him. Within a week, several hundred of the smartest humans ever to live were at his side, plotting the end of the *Out* rebellion. Some were willing. Others were not. But with his huge stature and inelegant forcefulness, Gerrard made them all listen. It was easy for him to communicate, considering that after years of being jacked-*In*, everyone in the room spoke every language in the world.

"We can't fight as we've done in the past," he lectured them. "The *Outs* are burning our fields while we sleep, reprogramming our bots to poison us while we dream, and taking advantage of our unwillingness to *wake up*. We outnumber them a thousand to one, and they're using it against us. They know most of us would rather take our chances and stay jacked-in than un-jack and fight a battle street-to-street.

"But that all changes now."

"How?" argued Thiago Enici, an astrophysicist so thin he looked skeletal. "They're scattered everywhere. We don't have enough automatons. And every time they capture one of our weapons, they assume it into their arsenal."

"He's right," said the masterful psychologist, Sara Von Berlitz. Sara was known to everyone in the room as the *Mind Mistress*, for her *In* world was a galactic-scale replica of a human brain. She knew the purpose of every neuron, and she understood what everyone would think before they thought it. "Attrition will be the end of us," Sara grinned a soulless grin. "But what Gerrard is saying, I believe, is that we should not work for the *destruction* of the *Outs*, but rather their *removal.*"

"Isn't that the same thing?" Thiago grimaced.

"Not at all," said Sara. "But I'll let Gerrard explain. He'll be less insulting than I would."

Gerrard steepled his fingers. Sara had been right, of course. She'd known what he'd been planning all along.

Forty three years of *In* had been more than enough. With most of humanity having limitless access to knowledge and the infinite ability to test and retest every scientific theory, the technological leaps had been vast. The gravity weapons deployed against the *Outs* were but a fraction of what the *Ins* had learned. They had mastered chemistry and unlocked the dark secrets of quantum mechanics, but more importantly they had invented higher forms of deep space travel. And although they had yet to test any of their new interstellar devices in the real world, it mattered little. Inside *In*, scientists had simulated millions of journeys into the cosmos.

"And it's time we put our brains to work," boomed Gerrard De Napoli. "The *Outs* know how this ends. They know we'll destroy them. They know their future holds only running, hiding, and dying."

"But they'll take thousands of us with them." Thiago Enici flexed his skinny fingers. "It could be any of us who dies next. Me...them...or even you."

Gerrard raised his chin, and Thiago fell silent.

"Exactly my point, Ser Enici. No matter how many weapons we forge, how many *Out* cities we raze, they'll get their victories. They'll kill twenty here, and two thousand there. But we've a way to stop it all."

"A cease-fire?" Thiago looked incredulous.

"Of sorts," said Gerrard. "We offer them a deal. They'll resist the notion at first. They'll suspect a trap. But they'll come around. Earth is ours now, and they know it. The only option they have is to leave."

"But where?" asked someone in the crowd.

"Does it matter?" Gerrard rolled his neck. "No. Not really. But if you ask every scientist here, they'll say the most likely candidate is Jupiter."

"We're sending them into Jupiter?" Thiago glowered.

"Not *into* it. *Around* it. It's not a trap, as you've supposed. We're not going to kill them. We'll make them a ship...a perfect one. Jupiter's hydrogen will fuel the micro-fusion reactors forever. We've done the tests. We know the answers. We'll make it elegant, beautiful, and powerful. And then we'll send them on their merry way. They'll have food forever. They'll have technology beyond their wildest dreams. But most importantly, they'll be gone. No more bombs laid in *In* towers. No more slaughters of the sleeping."

"You're a military strategist," Thiago argued. "No one here expected you to fight the *Outs* like this."

Gerrard looked proud of himself. "Wars are won in the mind," he said. "What happens on the battlefield is decided long before any soldier puts his boots on the ground."

"And if they refuse?" Thiago asked what everyone else in the room wanted to know.

"Then we'll lose a few hundred thousand," Sara Von Berlitz stepped forward again. "And they'll lose everyone. It's a moral option, Thiago. What's the phrase they used to use? The *Outs* will have to take it…or *leave* it."

Waking Rafe

When Rafe sat up in his breather chair and gazed at the people surrounding him, the first thing he remembered hearing them say was, "You're different, son."

"Where am I?" he murmured.

From somewhere in the mass of people crowding the tiny room, he heard someone answer. "Alta Sur." The woman craned her neck to see him. "Near the fault-line."

"But don't worry, kid," a squat, sweaty man blurted. "Fault's been contained. Gravity pods. No earthquakes here, not unless the *Outs* make 'em."

Rafe swung his legs over the side of the breather chair. His feet hurt. His eyes hurt. He felt tired for a reason he couldn't fathom. He looked at his hands and at the people crowding him in. Everything about the room, the crowd, even his skin felt dirty. An hour ago he'd been floating wraithlike through a thousand corridors of time and space.

And now this.

A man in a white lab-coat walked up to him. His collar was stained and his hair greasy.

Never seen anyone so filthy before, thought Rafe. *Everyone and everything...unclean.*

"How do you feel?" the man in the lab-coat asked. "The chairs are better than ever, but even so...most people say they feel sticky for a week or two. And your eyes will probably hurt, too. When they peel the retinal pads off, it tends to sting for a few days. But your muscles…your body…those should be fine. Especially for you, Rafe. Your jacks were state of the art."

"I'm hungry," was all he could muster.

The room laughed at that. It felt like they were watching him, judging him. During his two decades of being jacked-in, he had studied all the Berlitz rules of human psychology, and in his mind he remembered all the emotional challenges of un-jacked.

Doesn't matter.

Knowing it…not the same as feeling it.

Because this is the real world.

Isn't it?

"What's the matter, kid?" The squat man stared at him. "You sick? Maybe you're not who they say you are. Happens all the time. Geniuses in the ether ain't shit out here."

"No," he said. "I'm really just hungry, is all."

In silence, he counted the people in the room. *Nineteen. In a room made for just one. What do they want?*

After another breath, he knew he'd been un-jacked. He'd consumed all the history books. He knew this room was one of billions in the real world. The only thing he couldn't figure was; *why'd they pull me out?*

Why me?

Why now?

The man in the lab-coat touched his arm. The sensation was unlike anything he'd ever felt. Sure, he'd been touched thousands of times in the ether. At the ripe age of twelve, he'd spent five months drowning in an ocean of sex. Even though five months was far less than most boys spent, he knew what being touched was supposed to feel like.

And this isn't it.

"Sorry." The man recognized his discomfort. "It was the same for me. Look, let's get you downstairs. They've got some food for you...*real* food. It might hurt to swallow at first, but you'll manage."

He had questions. He kept them locked away. The small crowd took him into their midst and led him to an elevator. The last elevator he'd used had been capable of delivering him to twelve-thousand different points in space and time. This one just had numbers.

Two-hundred twenty numbers.

"Floors," explained the rail-thin woman standing behind him. "We're in a tower. Each number goes to a different one."

Only two-hundred and twenty, he thought. *Now I know I've been un-jacked.*

The elevator took him up. On the two-hundred nineteenth floor, he stepped out onto a hard, shiny marble surface. Three silver automatons looked him and his escorts over. He'd learned about the bots, of course. They were caretakers *and* guardians, fitted with enough medicines to cure any ailment a jacked-in user might develop...and armed with enough weapons to destroy a city.

And all for no reason.

He let the crowd guide him down a hallway. As he went, the number of escorts dwindled. Some walked into rooms adjacent to the hall. Others fell behind and whispered. At the hallway's end, only five remained: the man in the lab coat, the fat man, the tall, thin woman, a bald man in a grey sweater, and a beautiful but unsmiling woman.

The bald man opened the door for him. "Trencher," he announced. "My name. Go in and sit down. If you get dizzy, let us know. The bots have injections for that."

Trencher, he committed the man's name to memory. He remembered learning that people used to have multiple names, names given by their family, names with some attachment to their bloodline.

Trencher. He looked at the shine on the bald man's head. *Made-up. He's never dug a hole in his life.*

The room beyond the door was different than all the others he had glimpsed. Every surface was covered in membrane screens, and wheeling stars burned brightly on all of them. It looked like outer space, only not really.

"We thought it'd make you more comfortable." Trencher followed him in. "We hear you like to spend your learning-time floating in the stars."

"Yes," he murmured. *But it's too obvious this is a room, and not deep space. I can see the gaps between the screens. How old is this tech? A thousand years?*

He sat at a table that appeared to hover in the empty black between a million stars. Sitting down felt somehow more natural than walking. Even though his jacks had trained his muscles to stand, walk, and do everything his body had never really done, *sitting just feels right.*

Trencher sat beside him, and the man in the white lab-coat slid into the chair opposite him. Soon everyone was sitting, and they all looked infinitely more relaxed than moments ago.

"I'm Toggle. Professor Toggle, if you like," said the man in the lab-coat. "This here is Emperor." He looked at the short, fat man. "And this is Silk," he said with a gesture at the thin woman. "And this...well...this is Absinthe." He glanced fearfully at the beautiful, frowning woman. "We're all scientists to some degree, of course. But Absinthe's perhaps a little more dedicated than the rest of us."

He looked at all of them.

Emperor...well...we know what his world is like.

Silk. She looks tired.

Toggle. Obvious he'd rather not be here.

Absinthe. I'd have trouble dreaming anyone prettier.

Toggle let him think it over for a moment, then pushed a bowl of pale gruel in front of him. "Sorry," the Professor said again. "Everything here's gruel. No need for anything else. Try it. It's not so bad."

He spooned two scoops into his mouth, swallowed, and rubbed his throat. In the ether, nothing had ever tasted anything less than transcendent. He didn't have a word to describe how bland the gruel was.

"Rafe," said Trencher, "Do you know where you are?"

"Alta Sur," he remembered. "Silk already said. Used to be called Calif-ornia, or something like that."

Trencher shook his head. "That's not what we mean. What we mean is—"

"You un-jacked me."

"That's right."

"And now I'm *Out*. For some reason, you plucked me from the middle of my research. I'd just split myself up to exist in five different times. I was in heaven, and you decided *today* was the right time to cut the cord and bring me to a room filled with fake stars and tasteless food."

"You're angry?" Trencher looked worried.

"No. Not really. I just…I just don't know what all these *feelings* are. I've heard others tell me. But all the sensory jacks in the world can't prepare anyone for this."

"What do you feel?"

He looked his arms up and down. When he looked back up, Absinthe was staring at him. "Itchy," he said. "Heavy."

After slicking back his oily hair, Emperor smirked at him. "They say you spend most of your time in zero-G. Wasn't too smart, was it, Rafe? Your jacks got used to it. Your muscles got floppy. You should've dreamed yourself someplace on the ground. Where there's gravity, you know."

He disliked Emperor already. "There's plenty of gravity in deep space," he said.

"Not the right kind. Not enough for your jacks to train you," Emperor grunted.

"I didn't think I'd ever leave."

Emperor snorted. Toggle pulled the bowl of gruel away. Absinthe kept staring, burning a hole right through him with her glass-blue eyes.

"*No one* wants to come *Out*," reasoned Trencher. "We understand. Our first times were just as hard. It's only been a month, and we're dying to get back *In*. Literally dying. They pulled thirty of us *Out*. Only nineteen are left."

A month? Eleven dead? He looked at them with more respect than moments ago, even Emperor.

"Why?"

"It's a long story," said Trencher. "We'll tell you tomorrow. First we want you to eat. Then clean up. Then sleep. Real sleep. As in sleep in a bed. And when you wake up, we'll bring you back here and show you everything."

"I don't want to sleep."

"First rule of being *Out*," said Silk, "you have to sleep. You'll go mad without it. Or maybe you'll die."

"How do I do it?"

Trencher nodded to the far end of the table. "Absinthe will show you."

They left him, all of them except Absinthe. The room felt better in their absence, somehow closer to the silence he liked to dwell in. He closed his eyes and pretended the stars floating on the membrane screens were real. He almost felt himself falling through the void, endless and serene.

Like home.

"Try all you want. It won't work," she said to him.

When he opened his eyes, Absinthe was sitting much closer than before. Her eyes looked like the ice of Saturn's rings, the frost of a dusty blue nebula. He'd never seen anything so *human* before.

"What won't work?" he asked.

"Imagining yourself back *In*. Wishing yourself out of this place. They say we used to do something called *dreaming*. We'd go to sleep at night. We'd touch other places and be other people. Not anymore. In the ether, why do this dreaming? Pointless."

"Why are you telling me this?" He felt something in his belly. *Fear? Is that what they call it?*

"Because when you go to sleep tonight, you'll die a little death. You won't dream. You won't touch another world. You won't have any control. You'll fall into darkness and you'll think you're dead. And it might be you *will* die. Maybe. We'll see."

"Wait…" His fear felt thicker now. "You mean…I might die while I sleep?"

She smiled at last. It didn't make her prettier, as he'd expected. The turn of her lips looked cruel. Like a star dying.

"It's not the sleep that'll kill you, Rafe. Now come with me. I'm taking you to your room. And no, we aren't going to make love. Not out here in this disgusting place."

"Oh." He stood with her. For the first time in his life, he felt stupid. *Did I expect sex to happen? Why would she say that?*

"There will be monitors, of course." She led him to the room's far end, opposite the door he'd entered by. When she placed her palm on the wall, the stars dwindled. A section of membrane screens slid aside, revealing the colorless hallway beyond. "And there'll be bots. They'll look scary. But they won't hurt you. I'm sure you did your studying. They're here to protect you."

"Well…yes, but—"

"Good." She walked into the hallway and touched the wall. A white panel moved. In the room behind the panel lay a lamp, a small table with a pitcher of water, and a flat, soft-looking square on the floor.

"Is that—"

"A bed?" she answered. "Yes. You lie down on it. You close your eyes. You'll probably wet yourself in the night. In the table drawer you'll find spare clothes."

"Wet myself?"

"Piss your pants." She looked disgusted. "It's normal. Sensory jacks train muscle control, but not urge containment. If you can manage it, relieve yourself across the hall. We don't have toilets, of course. Just holes in the floor that go all the way down. Shower yourself afterward. If you get confused, just ask the bot."

It was too much, too fast. He'd always reasoned himself to be highly intelligent. He'd created galaxies broader in scope and finer in detail than all the other people he'd met in the ether.

But out here I'm an idiot.

Absinthe must have guessed what he was thinking. She smiled again, her lips twisting.

She hates me, he thought as she left him alone in the dark. *And I hate this place.*

He'd have fallen asleep if not for the bot standing in the corner.

The chrome thing glinted even in the impossibly low light. He watched it, and it watched him. It stood a full head taller than him. It had four arms, three legs, and a curved arch of silver steel resembling a neck. It had no real head, only three little red orbs atop its neck. It looked graceful. And dangerous.

Eyes, he imagined. *Watching me. Waiting for something.*

He stretched out on the bed.

He forgot the world and plunged into darkness.

* * *

When he woke, he felt more new sensations. He blinked, and his vision blurred. He stretched, and his arms were loose and weak.

Worse yet, he was still hungry.

Took two spoons' worth. How much more was I supposed to eat?

He staggered to his feet. After he stretched, yawned, and rolled his shoulders a half-dozen times, his body began to feel like it had yesterday. *Sticky, but alive.*

The bot looked at him. Its red-orb eyes bobbed on its chrome-steel neck. It looked fully ready to carve him to tatters.

"Shower, sir?" it asked him.

"Shower?"

"You're dirty, sir."

He regarded himself. *Of course I'm dirty*, he wanted to say. *I was never dirty in the ether. I—*

His pants were soaked through. The shirt he'd worn to bed clung to his stomach, damp and cold.

Absinthe was right.

For all the sensations of the real world he disliked, showering wasn't one of them. He stood under a sleek chrome nozzle behind a glass screen, and savored the feeling of warm water cascading over his skin. Each droplet felt sublime, the soft rain unlike anything he'd dreamed for himself in the ether. He wanted to stand beneath the water forever. It was the closest thing to being jacked-*In* he'd felt since being unplugged.

Surrounded by feeling.

This is more like it.

I wonder where Absinthe is.

When the bot chirped a command and the stream of warm water stopped, he plummeted back to reality. No matter that the bot gave him a warm towel and fresh, clean-looking white shirt and pants, he lost the shower's saturating warmth. His cold, chrome-steel friend instructed him how to dress himself. And then it led him out into the hallway and toward the room covered in membrane screens.

When he arrived, the walls were stars again. The ceiling and floor swam with white pinpricks against oceans of black. At a long table, a bowl of gruel and a cup of water awaited him. He ignored the five sitting people. He collapsed in his chair and shoveled every spoonful of pale fluid into his mouth. They murmured a few questions, but he heard nothing as he gulped down his breakfast.

"When you're *In*, eating's more fun," grunted Emperor. "Meats that melt in your mouth. Spirits you can drink to numb your boredom and make sex feel all the better. It's easier, ain't it, Rafe? To have a bot shoot gruel into your gut…and all the while you're thinking it's a feast?"

After the last drop slid into his belly, he felt better. He looked up to see the same five who'd been in the room yesterday: *Emperor, Professor Toggle,*

Silk, Trencher, and Absinthe. He envied them, for they seemed so comfortable with the real world. He hated them all a little bit, *except Absinthe*.

"How do you feel today, Rafe?" Toggle looked concerned. You slept twelve hours. That's unusual."

"How long was I supposed to sleep?" he asked.

"About nine, maybe ten."

"Usually the first night is less," added Silk.

"I don't know why, but I was tired." He looked at all of them. "I'd been so busy. I'd just made four new worlds, and I'd stopped time in three of them so I could study the fourth. It was my thesis, you know, for acceptance into the Illusarium. I wanted to study macro-evolution, but—"

"Yes, we know," Trencher cut in. "We know all about you, Rafe. We're *from* the Illusarium. We were teachers. You don't remember us, of course. But we remember you."

"Teachers? All of you?"

"Yes…well…all of us except *her*." Emperor gestured at Absinthe. "She's from somewhere else."

"I'm ready." He looked at all of them.

"Ready for what?" Emperor smirked. "More gruel?"

Silk rolled her eyes. "Don't be an asshole, Emp. Rafe's done everything we've asked of him. It's time."

"Are we sure?" asked Toggle.

Rafe looked at Absinthe. He expected her approval, maybe even her disgust, but she gave him nothing. She batted her beautiful eyelashes, but her mouth never moved.

"I'm ready," he said again.

Everyone except Absinthe traded glances. Somehow, even though he'd never really seen what doubt did to a human face, he understood.

Another new sensation.

My neck feels hot.

Is this anger?

"Either tell me why I'm here or jack me back *In*."

It was Silk who answered. She steepled her skinny fingers, clenched her narrow jaw, and let out a breath like a distant planet dying.

"We need your help, Rafe," she began. "And when I say 'we', I don't just mean the five of us sitting here in this room. I mean everyone. I mean humanity."

She let it sink in for a few seconds. Again he looked at Absinthe. She was gazing off into the starlit membrane screens. *Not even listening.*

"What's the last thing you remember?" Silk asked him.

"Um…well…I already told you. I'd just finished making a new planet. It was one of four. All inhabitable. With organics, with life. But all different. I'd frozen time in the other three. I was going to seed each one with different forms of basic life. Carbon-based. Silicon-based. Etcetera. My plan…well…my dream was to start time on each planet at the same exact time. I'd speed time up so life would evolve quickly, but then I'd slow it down to study it at different points."

"And you designed this simulation, this program, all based on the science you've learned?" said Toggle. "No cheating to save certain life-forms and kill others off? You based it all on *Out* physics, didn't you?"

"Obviously." Absinthe finally said something. "He wouldn't be here otherwise."

Toggle ignored her. "What about the time-compression device you made? You didn't have to make a device, you know? You could've just imagined a few made-up physics to stop and accelerate time, couldn't you have? Just to make it easier."

"Yes...well," he stammered. "If I'd have done that, it would've felt...I don't know...fake."

"Fake!" laughed Emperor. "In the ether, *everything's* fake. Or everything's real. It doesn't matter!"

"I made the device because I wanted to. I don't know why. It wasn't part of my thesis. I wanted to study evolution. To see everything."

"To know if every world would end up in *In*." Emperor's smile faded.

"No," he said. "I didn't assume any endings at all. These were my worlds. I didn't let anyone else see them. I didn't want any contamination. I just wanted to know."

"But *we* saw them," said Trencher.

"How? You hacked in?"

"Not exactly." Emperor made a face.

My neck's hot again.

I'm angry. Again.

"What else did you watch?" He glared at them. "Is it all a big lie? Does the Illusarium nose around everything everyone does? Do you spy on people having sex? Do you cheat and create your own worlds based on whatever everyone else is doing?"

Toggle touched his shoulder. Something inside him became calmer. He hated his body for reacting to it. That other people could change his mood felt like a betrayal.

"Rafe," began Toggle, "it's not like that. *In*'s all part of one big system. Some worlds are tucked away in the farthest corners of the system, but no one can disconnect completely. So when someone does something different, something special, everyone else feels it. It's like a tremor, like a faraway star exploding. You don't see it right away. But you feel it. You sense it."

"But my worlds weren't special," he argued. "Other people have done evolutionary experiments. Other people made planets, too."

Silk craned her neck to stare at him. "It isn't your worlds we care about, Rafe. Not even that you made four of them. Not even that you applied *Out* physics to their creation."

"So...what *do* you care about?" he shot back.

"Your device," she said.

"What about it?"

She shook her head at him. He wasn't sure what that meant.

"It works," she said.

"I know," he blurted. "Like Absinthe said, '*obviously*.'"

"No, we mean it works everywhere. The *Out* physics you used to make it are perfect. It's *real*, Rafe."

"What do you mean, *real*?"

Everyone looked to Absinthe. He didn't grasp the meaning at first. But when she put her palms on the table and batted her eyelashes, all the while looking deadly serious, he understood.

Everyone's waiting for her to talk.

"We built your little time-compression toy," she told him. "It works. *In* there. *Out* here. It works."

"You mean...for real?" he said. "But why? Why'd you build it? And if you'd already stol—, I mean...copied it, why'd you un-jack me?"

This time, Absinthe didn't bat her eyelashes. She looked at him, carving her way into his consciousness. He felt smaller than he'd ever felt before.

"Because the *Outs* are coming, you simple boy. And we need you to help us kill them all."

Moz and the Achilles

Moz punched the two-hundred pound bag one last time.

It nearly ruptured from the impact. It swung from its chain for what felt like an eternity, misshapen from the blow.

He felt good today. *Really good.* Sweat dripped from his forehead and pattered on the floor. His gloves, black and tattered, felt like extensions of his fists. He looked at himself in the training room's only mirror. He was six-foot five of gleaming, ebon muscle, his silver tattoos winding snakelike down his arms. He felt like a god. As huge as the moon Ganymede. As powerful as Jupiter itself.

I'm ready, he thought. *I'm next. Send me tomorrow. I'll finish it in a day.*

But when Anjel knocked on the glass door and walked into the room, all his thoughts of fighting evaporated.

Anjel was his opposite. Lily white as pale sand, her eyes greener than anything in existence, she took long, ethereal strides across the room. She wore only two strips of grey fabric, just enough to exercise in, but no more. She was tall, lithe, and thin as a sword turned on its edge. He hoped for a kiss, for a smile, for anything, but she made her way to the racks and pulled the smallest set of boxing gloves onto her fists without so much as glancing at him.

"You started without me." She sized up the huge punching bag.

"I *finished* without you," he chuffed.

She grinned, and like a striking serpent hit the bag three times. For all Moz's size, *she's faster*.

"You know," she said between pinpoint jabs, "if you'd waited, I could've given you a real workout." She drilled the bag's bottom with a knifelike kick. "Something better than all this punching."

He shivered at that. He remembered why it was so easy to forget everything when he was with her.

"Yeah. I know," he said. "I've got no excuses. Not even gonna try."

She hit the bag with a roundhouse kick, and he swore it swung back on its chain as far as when he'd slugged it. "Good." She eyed him. "I hate it when you lie."

That stung a little. "Lie?" He crossed his massive arms. "I never lie. Not to you."

She hit the bag with three elbows and sent it spinning with a hard knee-kick. "Never?" she said. "Maybe not with your mouth. But I know you're not thinking about *me*. Not today."

"Well I wasn't. I mean…not before you got here. But now I am."

She put her hands on her hips. "Just ask," she said.

"Ask what?" He pretended not to know.

"C'mon, Moz. Just ask."

"Ok. Fine. Are they back?"

She nodded, and his smile could've split the sun in half.

"Yeori came back first," she said. "I thought he'd never make it. You know…because he's old. But he made it. He was covered in dust. I've never seen so much."

"Dust?" He was confused. "From what?"

She smiled. "From all the rubble. C'mon, Moz. Don't be stupid. You didn't think it'd be clean, did you? Back there isn't like it is out here. Everything's rock and plastic and old, old metal. Yeori made a mess. He looked like hell. But his suit's just fine. And so's he."

Damn. The old man. Back first. If he can do it…

"What about Kosi and Zamo?"

"The brothers?" She shrugged. "Just as good. They came back second. For a minute we thought the *Ins* would come through after them. But it was like Yeori said. '*Nothing left. No bots. No tanks.*'" Even the quake-bombs couldn't stop them.

Moz pounded one fist into the other. If he'd felt good before Anjel had come, *now I'm in heaven.*

"Can we go see them?" He tore off his gloves and dropped them on the floor.

"Of course," she sighed. "Why do you think I'm here?"

He ran to his room. In minutes, he dressed. When he burst back into the slender hallway beyond his door, he was almost disappointed to see Anjel had covered up in her usual white shawl.

No. It's good, he thought. *No distractions. Today's all about the war.*

She walked. He followed. He'd been down the Achilles' labyrinthine hallways thousands of times, but hadn't walked this fast since he'd been a little boy. The silver walls shined as always they did. The floors felt like glass beneath his sandals, giving a little under each of his footfalls. *Beautiful*, he thought. *Just like Anjel.*

And the Achilles *was* beautiful.

The ship was perfection, the only thing he imagined was equal to Anjel. He'd lived in it since birth, and he'd run its every long, twisting corridor. He'd gazed out its windows for days, wondering what it'd be like to swim in the scarlet broth of Jupiter's never-ending storms. He'd done spacewalks to learn how the grav-drives operated, and he'd marveled at the Achilles' spiraling black arms, its spiderlike limbs stretching for miles into empty space. As a child he'd wondered who had made such a thing, so vast and flawless and terrifying, but his heart had broken when he learned who. And why.

No time for that today. He shoved all his old memories out. *Today's for settling scores.*

After walking down three long, curled hallways and crossing through a huge, empty grav-chamber, he and Anjel arrived. She tapped a chrome door with her fingertip, and the sheaf of metal slid aside. The room beyond was an elbow joining two of the Achilles' limbs.

Within awaited Yeori, white as a ghost and smiling.

And Kosi, dark as ash and big as a baby meteor.

And Zamo, even bigger.

But most impressive of all was Frigg, the Achilles' Master of Weapons, and the one man Moz looked up to.

Others were in the room, too. Almost invisibly, the scientists, medics, and curious observers sat in a distant ring around the grav-hub in the room's center. *Must be a hundred here,* thought Moz. But they were all silent, painted on the outer walls, their gazes fixed on the three warriors who'd just returned.

Moz took the lead ahead of Anjel. When he got to the grav-hub, Yeori was talking.

And everyone was listening.

"…hit the last tower in the city." Yeori waved his powder-covered hands. "It was huge. Three big bots came for me. They had quake-bombs. But when they shot 'em up, it gave me time to recalibrate. I went light. *Really* light. Two kilos or so. I jumped so high that by the time the bombs chewed up the earth, I landed like a feather right 'tween the bots. Then I went heavy. *Really* heavy. Eight-thousand kilos. I hit one bot so hard he fell apart like glass. And then I threw the second one into the third. Was good for me I did'na hit the third with my fists. He still had one quake-bomb left. Would'a broke my suit, leastways."

"What about the tower?" Frigg boomed.

"Well…" Yeori said with his strange, old world accent, "I tried expressing some grav on it, but the *Ins*…there must'a been some important ones inside. They had plexi-walls. They learn quick, the bastards. But there ain't no plexi-wall can take a punch from a ten-thousand kilo Yeori. I hit it in each of its six corners. Damn thing came down on top of me. Some of stuck to me…you know…me bein' so heavy. But after it settled, I went to eleven-thousand kilos and pushed my way out."

"Eleven-thousand kilos?" Frigg grimaced. "Risky. Enough particulates and *boom*…you'd have become a singularity."

"Bah!" Yeori scoffed.

"How many *Ins*?" Zamo grunted.

"Eight…nine-thousand in the tower." Yeori shrugged. "Hard to tell. They fell like rocks, you know. But they made no craters. Only splats. Lots of red."

"I wonder if they felt anything," Moz heard Anjel murmur. He swore she almost looked sad.

Nah, not her, he decided.

Frigg looked at all three warriors. They'd taken off their suits since returning, but Moz could still picture them ready for war. *Dressed all in grey. Sleek as Saturn's rings.*

Heroes.

Finally, Frigg dismissed them. The three warriors looked exhausted. Zamo and Kosi whacked Moz affectionately on the shoulder as they lumbered past. Yeori stopped long enough to mutter, "Careful what you wish for, Mozelle. Death down there ain't like it is up here."

The old man ambled through a door on the room's far side. Moz wondered what he'd meant.

In moments, the watchers on the outer walls shuffled away. Men and women dressed in blacks and whites vanished into dozens of doors. Soon all was silent, and he, Anjel, and Frigg were the only ones left.

"Moz." Frigg came to him. "Been to the training room, I see. Looking huge."

Frigg looked him up and down. He was like a father to Moz, *always has been*. He was strapping and dark-skinned, a giant amongst the Achilles' men. His eyes were the shade of Jupiter's darkest moons, two storms waiting to begin.

We even look alike.

Sometimes I wonder.

"Moz's been preparing," offered Anjel. "In and out every cycle. Works almost as hard as I do."

Frigg nodded, but didn't smile. "I know. I've heard. But he also knows lifting all the iron in the world won't matter when a quake-bomb's headed his way. Or when he miscalculates his kilos and buries himself twenty clicks deep in the earth. Or if—"

"I know all that," Moz finally interrupted.

"Yes," Frigg grunted. "You do."

With a glance at Anjel and a hard stare at Frigg, he asked the question he'd wanted to all along:

"Is it ready?"

"The fourth suit?" Frigg crossed his arms.

"Yeah."

"Ready as ever."

"Well?" He felt his heart pounding.

Frigg looked at him. Moz was the bigger man, but Frigg's gaze weighed down on him, heavier than everything. "We've had the talk," Frigg began. "I won't lecture you again. If you say you're ready—"

"I *am* ready," he declared.

Frigg nodded, serious as Jupiter's red eye. "Fine. Come to the Thorax Room tomorrow. And I'll teach you how not to die."

"You mean you'll show me how to crush the *Ins*."

"No. I mean I'll show you how not to die."

Frigg had said it a dozen times before, but now more than ever Moz felt it was true. Frigg walked away, leaving him and Anjel standing there alone. *What's he always say?* he tried to remember. *Breaking buildings is easy. Killing hundreds of thousands is hard. Not dying is even harder.*

But going through the Door for the very first time is hardest.

* * *

The next cycle, Moz woke early.

He sat up in his bed and watched Anjel doze beside him. She had pushed off her sheets in the night, and now her body lay naked for him to admire. He smiled at her, envious. *Milk in the moonlight*, Yeori had once remarked of her skin. He didn't know exactly what that meant. All he knew was; no matter all the challenges of existing without the rhythms of day and night, she'd always slept deeper than anyone he'd known.

Clear conscience, he told himself.
Pure heart.

He dressed in all black, but left his boots behind as Frigg had instructed. Leaving without waking Anjel, he took to the Achilles' halls. The walk to the Thorax Room would take him half an hour. He didn't mind. He needed time to think, to reflect, to prepare to become the fourth and final warrior in the campaign against the *Ins.*

He dwelled on it as he walked. In its long, slow orbit around Jupiter, the Achilles housed approximately eleven-thousand men, women, and children. Most were engineers, scientists, and laborers, and were crucial to the Achilles' upkeep. He'd once heard that all the technology employed to keep the vast space station viable had been taught to his people by the *Ins*. He'd never believed it. He believed what most everyone else did: *The Ins sent us out here with just enough resources to last a single generation. They wanted us to die out. They wanted Earth all for themselves.*

We don't need them.

Never did.

By the time he reached the Thorax Room, he'd worked himself into a foul mood. In the massive Thorax, largest of all the Achilles' chambers, he stomped past dozens of engineers, ignoring everyone watching him. He came to Frigg, who stood alone with Yeori. The two were in deep discussion.

And so he waited.

"…had better work," he could hear Yeori saying. "The three…I mean *four* of us could spend a hundred years breaking a new city every day. Won't be enough."

As ever, Frigg stood with his huge arms crossed. "There are some who think the *Ins* will offer a truce. If they do, we can carve out a space big enough to colonize, and we leave them alone ever after."

"Yeah?" Yeori scoffed. "Some believe it. But not *you*. You know what'll happen. In a hundred years they'll have every square inch covered with jack-towers. And in a thousand, every planet in every galaxy will be teemin' with *In* servers. They don't even have to touch each other to breed, you know. They just dream it, and the bots pop out another little devil. You think they'll leave us alone when all we're doing is taking up space?"

"It occurred to me they might want the Achilles back," Frigg sighed. "Not that they couldn't make another for themselves. But if they ever found out the upgrades we've managed, they might come for us."

"Or just send off more missiles than we can shoot down." Yeori made a face. "The K bombs. Kill us all off. Leave the ship lookin' pretty as ever."

Moz worried the two men might talk forever, but as soon as he thought it, Yeori looked his way.

"I hope you're ready." The pallid old man ambled past him. "War's a young man's game. Soon you'll need to fight well enough for you *and* me."

He watched the old man walk away, but said nothing. He'd learned not to let Yeori get under his skin. After all, the old man was Anjel's grandfather.

Which meant that more than anyone else besides the *Ins*, *he doesn't like me*.

"Moz." Frigg shook his hand once Yeori was gone. The Achilles' Weapons Master had a handshake strong enough to rattle anyone. Big as he was, Moz felt it.

"Where's the suit?" He needed to know.

"Not yet," said Frigg. "First come with me."

His heart sank a little, but he didn't let it show. *If I pout, Frigg will find someone else to win the war.*

Frigg waved at him to follow. He fell in alongside his mentor. He liked the way the engineers working in the vast room stopped what they were doing to watch. He heard their whispers, and he felt proud.

"That's Mozelle, the next warrior," he heard them say.

"Look how huge he is."
"He'll be a hero soon."

By the time Frigg led him to a tiny, glass-walled room on the Thorax Room's perimeter, he was bursting with anticipation. He knew Frigg would see it, but he didn't much care.

"Sit down," said Frigg.

He sank into a silver chair.

Frigg closed the glass door and tapped a panel. The walls, ceiling, and floor went opaque. The heavy black blotted out the lights from the Thorax Room. Moz could only see by the glimmer of a lonely blue lamp in the corner.

Frigg stood before him, more serious than ever he'd seen. "Before we get started, I've a history lesson for you," the Weapons Master said.

"You know I've studied." Moz shrugged. "I know why we're doing this. You don't need to—"

"Do you know who Achilles was?" Frigg interrupted him.

He didn't understand. He leaned forward in his chair. "Who? You mean the ship? *Our* ship, right? Not a who. A *what*."

Frigg looked disappointed. "Listen, Moz. Don't talk. Just listen. I know what you believe. I know what everyone believes. But there're things you need to know before you do this."

"Ok. I'm listening."

Frigg uncrossed his arms. "If you ask almost anyone on this ship why we're using the Door to slip onto Earth and fight the *Ins*, they'll tell you the same thing. They'll say it's because we want our home back. They'll say Earth belongs to us as much, if not

46

more than, the jacked-in hordes. And maybe they were right, *a few hundred years ago*. But those of us who know the truth know that the Earth isn't ours anymore. We left it, Moz. And we left it willingly. Our ancestors could've stayed and fought, but they bargained to come out here. And now the Achilles is home. It's what *is*, not what could be."

"I don't think I understand." Moz hadn't expected this. "What are you saying? We're stopping the war?"

"Not hardly." Frigg's face darkened. "I just want you to know the real reason we're doing it."

"Good." He looked at Frigg and saw a shadow he didn't ever remember seeing before. "Because for a second it sounded like you were saying we've got no good reason to fight."

"Oh we've got a good reason, Moz. The best reason. You see, Achilles was what they used to call a Myrmidon. He was a hero of war, a god among warriors back when wars were fought man-to-man, sword against sword. It's kind of what Yeori is, kind of what you'll soon be. But Achilles had a weakness he didn't know about. A fatal weakness. And because of it, all his strength didn't matter."

"So *we* have a weakness?"

"*Had*," Frigg stressed.

"I still don't get it."

Frigg sucked in a deep breath. "The *Ins* made this station, Moz. You know that. Everyone knows that. Maybe a few hundred years from now, we'll forget. But for now, most of us remember. Thing is, they gave it a weakness…just like Achilles. A flaw. And it wasn't something passive like not giving us enough resources or holding back technology. Most of the *Ins* wanted us to survive. They weren't evil, just indifferent. But some of them, and I mean the worst of them, plotted to kill us all. If not for a few brave geniuses aboard this ship, we'd be powder floating in Jupiter's atmosphere."

Moz felt his blood heat up. "How?"

"Decaying orbit. You know what that means?"

"Yeah."

"It was subtle, Moz. Very subtle. But we found it. They put a tiny subroutine into the Achilles' computers. Our ship wasn't called the Achilles back then. It was the Exemoni. It looked a lot different, too. Smaller. Not nearly as powerful. An *In* named Berlitz…she was the one who did it. She lied to her *In* comrades, lied to *everyone*. She ordered her scientists to infiltrate the Exemoni's construction and add the subroutine in. Decaying orbit. One quiet click every few months. Within a generation, we'd have all been dead."

Moz paled. "But we fixed it. Otherwise you and I would've never been here."

"Correct," said Frigg.

"And that was what…nine centuries ago? Vengeance for that would've been nice, but this woman and her friends…they're hundreds of years in their graves."

Frigg walked to the far end of the table and pressed his fists against the shining glass. "Not exactly, Moz."

"Not exactly? The *Ins* are immortal now? I think Yeori's proven that wrong…oh…about three-hundred thousand times."

Moz looked at him. "Not immortal. Not in the flesh anyway. They haven't figured that out yet. But what some of them did is just as bad. They programmed themselves into that damn imaginary world of theirs. Berlitz and a few hundred…they're like ghosts. They haunt the whole system. They preach to anyone who'll listen. 'The *Outs* are still a threat,' they whisper. 'They have to be ended.'"

"How? How do we know all this?"

"Damn, Moz. You really don't know, do you?" Frigg shook his head. "We still got *Outs* back on Earth. Not many, but enough. And they've been busy."

"Huh?" He looked at Frigg as though the big man had slapped him.

"They've been there all along. In the Krubera, they call it. In the caves. We've been piping signals to them for centuries, and they've been doing the same to us."

"The *Ins* haven't found them? How not?"

"I don't know," said Frigg. "I don't care. All I know is they've been down there since the beginning. Waiting. Helping. Stealing *In* technology. And building."

"Spies…" he exhaled.

"They built the Door, Moz. They knew this day would come. They built the Door and shot the instructions to us for opening it on our end. And the best part: the *Ins* still don't know they're there. The Krubera…the caves…the *Ins* have no clue. The fools are too busy dreaming to see what's sitting right under their noses."

It was too much, too quickly. He pulled his hands down his face and let the truth wash over him.

"What about what Yeori said?" he asked after a long silence. "About there being too many cities? The whole thing about even if there are four of us smashing *Ins* for the rest of our lives, we'll never get them all."

"It isn't about killing them all. Never was."

"It isn't?"

"No. It's about the servers. It's about the Berlitz persona. We have to smash every server she's on. She's the ultimate motivator, Moz. She's a sickness. She's a goddamn virus infecting every dreaming *In*. Without her, we hope they'll stop caring about us. We'll make a truce. Some of us will stay on Earth, and the rest of us will live here, on the Achilles. And we'll build more ships. And someday we'll find a planet of our own."

"Frigg, I—"

"I know. You had no idea. You thought we were gonna conquer the world and colonize it. But that ain't for us, Moz. The sun, the moon, the days and nights, the summers and winters…it's not for you and me. We're past that now. We belong to the Achilles. We belong out here in the stars."

"Damn." He hunkered in his chair and shook his head. "Now what?"

Frigg looked hard at him. The shadow passed. Story time was over.

"Now you get your ass out of that chair and out that door," the Weapons Master boomed. "And I show you how not to die."

A Sip of Absinthe

Rafe stood on an empty street.
The towers seemed to go on forever, lining each side of the long, barren highway, stretching to places unknowable between the clouds.

Everything was silent. The street looked as though it had been laid only yesterday, as though he were the first person ever to stand on its grey, glassy surface.

There was no wind.

There was no sound.

He was alone but for Absinthe.

God she's beautiful.

As though aware of his thoughts, she peered at him over her datapad. Her white dress was as spotless a thing he'd seen outside of *In*. Her eyes were bluer than the sky, but as devoid of emotion as the polished, lifeless street.

"You know how to use it, don't you?" she asked him.

He raised his left hand to eye-level. Locked around his wrist, the ebony bracer gleamed. "I never measured it like this." He squeezed the bracer, and the lone blue pip on its surface didn't move. "The way I did it, the whole thing glowed brighter the slower I made things go."

"Yes." She rolled her eyes. "Thing is; glowing is no good. If you don't slow things down enough and someone sees your wrist light up like some kind of star, they'll come for you. Anything that makes you easier to hit is bad."

He regarded himself. The black boots, grey pants, and deep blue cuirass they'd dressed him in made more sense now. *I'm the same color as the towers*, he thought. *But what happens if I leave the city?*

"So…" he said while turning his wrist, "…the more blue pips, the faster I'm going?"

"Correct," she said. "And the slower the rest of the world will seem."

He rolled his wrist. Tight against his skin, the bracer stayed still. "It's the same concept as in the ether? I just wish for it, and time speeds or slows depending on what I want?"

"No. Not even close." She shook her head. "First, it only works in *one* relativity mode. Speeds you up…slows everything else down. Never the reverse. We need you faster than the *Outs*, not slower. And second, there's no mind-link. You have to tap the blue pips with your finger. One tap slows everything by fifty percent. Two taps by seventy-five percent…and so on. It's exponential. Ten taps will make you go one-thousand twenty-four times faster than the world. Time will basically stop for everything a few inches off your skin. Don't even bother with fifteen taps. It'd be pointless."

"Oh." He felt stupid. "How do I make everything go normal? You know…me and the world at the same speed."

She smirked. "Tap it with two fingers at once. I'd do it in a quiet place if I were you. If you're in danger and you let everything catch up all at once, it'll leave you vulnerable. You'll be dizzy. You'll be *dead*."

He walked a few steps down the street and let it sink in. *They did it. They made it real.* In the ether he'd created the black bracer using laws of physics he'd never actually experienced in the flesh, *and now she's standing there telling me it really works.*

And she wants me to kill people with it.

He thought about how he'd made the device. The principles were rudimentary in theory, if not in execution. When he activated the band, his body and everything a few inches from his skin would be tricked. The band fooled his cells into thinking they were accelerating to near-light speeds. Everything away from his body would remain as-is, unaware of the tricks the band played, *slow and serene.*

"Relativity," he said mostly to himself.

"Yes." Absinthe walked up beside him. "Clever. Fool yourself. Fool the whole universe."

"Have you tried it? I mean…have *you* put the bracer on?"

She smirked. "No. Why would I? One glitch, and half your body will think it's going at light speed, while the other half stays slow. A real mess."

He didn't want to think about it. While in the ether he'd made the bracer so perfect it never failed, he didn't have any idea who'd replicated it in the real world. After a shudder, he tried instead to imagine what it would be like if they'd given it the opposite power.

"If you'd have reversed it, as in slowed *me* down, I could've just hidden away in some dark place. I could've turned it on and waited until the world ended. It would've felt like just a few minutes."

Absinthe frowned. "Cute. It's the second reason we didn't put the reverse power in."

He shrugged and looked up to the towers. It was easier than gazing at Absinthe. Even though during the last fourteen days he'd almost never seen her smile, she still melted him whenever she batted her long, pale eyelashes. One time when he'd awoken from an awful dream, she'd come to his door, and he'd almost kissed her.

Standing there in her nightclothes.
Hair messy from this thing they call sleep.
Cool as the water from…what do they call it?
The rain.

The towers, tall and magnificent as they were, looked small compared to the places he'd created in the ether. He'd made mountains tall enough to scrape the edge of space, oceans deep enough to devour planets. He tried, but he couldn't fully remember the places he'd made. They felt too far away.

They feel lost.

"Are you just going to stare at the sky all day?" She broke his reverie.

"No," he said glumly.

"Don't you want to try it?"

He glanced down to his wrist. He felt uneasy. And for a reason he didn't know, he couldn't tell Absinthe what he'd been thinking.

"I already know how it works," he said. "You told me. And you forget that I've slowed and sped up time more than anyone else…ever."

"Being cocky isn't for you, boy." Her glare was so cold it frosted his blood. "Nor will it serve you when the *Outs* start tearing down cities around you."

He looked at her, *finally*. He felt angry with her, and he hated that his heart was pounding, *my least favorite un-jacked feeling*. "I don't get it," he argued. "Why not send someone else? I mean…you already stole my creation before you un-jacked me. Why not make Trencher do it. Or even better, why not Emperor?"

She laughed at that. "You're cute. And stupid. Trencher is as weak as he is old. And Emperor, the fat slug, he's all talk. Hating the *Outs* isn't enough. Being young, fast, and knowing how to use your little bracelet is what it'll take."

"But—"

"We don't have time to train someone. Don't be dumb. Things don't last forever out here in the real world. The *Outs* have found a way back to Earth, and they're not going to wait for us to figure things out. They don't kill ten or twenty people at a time. They kill fifty thousand in a day. You hear me?" She narrowed her eyes. "You *understand*?"

I've never fought anyone in my life, he thought. *How can I start killing…just like that?*

"I know, I know." She waved her hand at him. "You never dreamed any conflict in your pretty, plugged-in world. It was just you, all alone, in your fancy paradise. Well it's simple. You kill a few *Outs* for me, and you go right back into the ether. We'll plug you in, and in a week's real-time your body'll forget it was ever out here in this…place."

"How many?" he asked.

"How many what?" She made a face.

"How many *Outs*? How many do I have to kill?"

She licked her lips. He swore he saw her smile. "Face-to-face? Only three. Three little *Outs*. Think you can manage it?"

"Just three? I don't—"

"That's what I said. Three. And then you'll do a little something after the three are gone. A little, simple something. And poof, the rest of the *Outs* will be gone. We'll jet you back here and we'll pop a few cables back in your brain. Your worlds are still loaded. It'll be like you never left."

"What little something?" He shivered.

"Worry about that later. Practice a little bit. Get used to using the bracelet in the real world. The next time an *Out* comes for a visit, you'll fly to him and get rid of him. You like being noble, don't you? Your psyche development said so. So how about saving the entire…fucking…planet? Would that be noble enough for you?"

Her tone had darkened word by word, and he didn't like it. Even so, he felt more important than a few minutes ago. He felt *convinced*. She knew which buttons to push in him. He didn't understand why he still wanted to like her.

"I heard Emperor talking about the bots." He looked away. "He said they use quake bombs and flechettes to kill *Outs*. Will I get some of those, whatever they are?"

Absinthe closed her eyes and shook her head, *disappointed*. "No, Rafe. You get to use this." She reached into a fold of her sterile white gown and produced a short little something. Then she pulled another something, a short, sharp-looking metal thing, out of the first something. It looked dangerous.

"What is that?" he asked.

"A knife." She licked her lips. "You stick it into the *Outs,* here, here, and here." She touched the knife's tip to his belly, his chest, and his throat. "And then you walk away as slow as you like."

He looked at the knife with a wide-open mouth. He felt chilled, his heart no longer thumping, but near to stopping.

"Oh, don't fret for the poor *Out.*" She slid the knife back into its protective something. "For him it'll feel like nothing. He'll die at the speed of light. It probably won't even hurt. It's cleaner than quake bombs, and a whole lot less painful than flechettes."

"I don't know if I can do it." He flexed his fingers and stared at his hands.

She sighed, a deep sigh. He'd never heard a sound like it before. He didn't know what to call it.

"Rafe, Rafe, Rafe." She came to him and touched his shoulder. "I know this is hard. I get it. I really do. But I need you to understand something, ok?"

He swam in the pale blue of her perfect eyes. Whatever she was doing with her voice, with her hand, *it's working.*

"The *Outs*…they want to hurt us," she continued. "Not just *some* of us. *All* of us. And it's like I told you. The bots have no chance against them. Believe me, if they did, we'd all just plug back in today. I'd come to visit your pretty world. You could show me the beautiful things you've made. We'd make love for days, weeks, however long we wanted. Life would be just as you've dreamed it: perfect."

Make love? He felt his resistance cracking. Hard, cold Absinthe was softening him up, her voice like water lapping up on the shores of *him*.

"But we can't plug in, Rafe. Not until we're safe," she said. "Do you remember the holo-vids Toggle showed you? Did you see the cities in ruin, the bodies on the streets?"

He nodded.

"Good. Because that's the work of just three little *Outs*. Three. And you remember what Toggle told you about their suits? You saw what they did? Heavy as a star's stomach in one breath, light as space-dust in the next. They can pulverize a tower with a few slaps. We thought about duplicating their suits, but instead we're betting on you. On *you*, Rafe." She held his gaze and squeezed his shoulder. "With your creation, you can be rid of them without leveling an entire city and killing thousands of people. You can do it clean. Quiet. And you can stop them before they make more suits. And before they send more men."

When she took her hand off his shoulder, he quaked from head to toe. It felt like she'd reached inside him and plucked his heartstrings. Until then, he hadn't even known he had heartstrings.

I know what I have to do, he thought.

Save. Everyone.

"Can I turn it on now?"

She smiled a true smile, the warmest thing he'd seen since they'd let him watch the sun come up for the first time. "Yes," she said. "But first, some rules."

"Rules?"

"Somewhere on these streets, we've hidden three dummies. You know what dummies are, right? Fake men. Big fake metal *Outs* dressed up for war. They don't move or anything, but they have sensors in their eyes. If they see you, you lose."

"How do I win?"

She smiled again. *Two in one day*, he thought.

"Each metal man has three soft spots." She pulled the knife back out and slid it out of its protective something. "Stick this into each soft spot and the metal man will fall to pieces."

"Sounds easy," he said.

He took the knife in his left hand and raised his wrist. He reached out to tap the ebony band and finish Absinthe's test at the speed of light, but she folded her fingers around his arm and pulled it down.

"Not *easy*," she said. "You're thinking you'll just stay fast. That you'll just turn your little toy all the way up and dance around the city while everything is frozen. You're thinking, 'Absinthe will blink her eyes once, and I'll be done in time to kiss her before she opens her eyes again.' Nope. Not so simple."

She was right. He had thought that. *All of it.*

"Well why can't I?" he asked. "I mean…that's the point, right? Just turn the bracer on and do all these things while everyone else is stuck going slow. Right?"

"You're going to get tired." She smirked.

"Tired?"

"Very tired. The human body, the *real* human body, isn't used to being tricked like this. A few minutes of running around, and you'll be gasping for breath. A few minutes more, and you'll be ready to sleep a whole day away. And if you fall asleep while the band is on, you'll die. Simple as that."

"It didn't work like that in the ether," he countered.

"We're not *in* the ether." She looked irritated. "You can't just flick your toy on and butcher everything. For one, that'd be foolish of us to allow. I mean...just think if the *Outs* stole the device. They'd kill the whole world in a few hours. But more importantly, it's just the way it is. The design, *your* design, exhausts its user at an exponential rate. We don't know why. It's like the universe's way of saying, 'You can borrow my power, but I'll be damned if you can keep it.'"

"So if I get tired, I should turn it off?"

"And hide until you recover," she added. "Remember; the *Outs* can level entire cities. If they find you, one little Rafe will be nothing."

He gulped. He'd never really been afraid before, *not like this*. Inside *In*, he'd never really learned about fear. He'd never had to.

"One more thing." Absinthe stared hard at him. "There's a vid-node and a tracker on the band. If you lose it...if it falls off or an *Out* takes it, it'll detonate. You know what detonate means, don't you?"

"Yes. It'll go *boom*."

She looked back to her datapad. "Right. So don't do anything...stupid."

* * *

That morning, on the streets of a city he didn't know, beneath silent towers stuffed to their tops with sleeping masses, he took Absinthe's test.

His first attempt, he walked away from Absinthe with the knife in his hand. Ten steps down the street, he glanced back.

Absinthe was gone.

I'm alone.

And just as he raised his wrist to tap the band, he heard a siren blaring.

"Failure!" the *Out* dummy screamed. "Restart!"

He hadn't even seen the thing. The metal dummy, seven feet tall and hiding in the towers' shadows, had been standing there all along.

I get it, he understood. *They think I'm not paying attention.*

I'll show them.

A bot skittered out of an alleyway, scooped up the dummy, and scurried out of sight.

Moving the dummy.

Never in the same place twice.

Get smart, Rafe.

Seven times, he tapped the black bracer with his index finger. He expected to hear a hum as a wave of relativity stole him away. He anticipated a vibration, a ping, *anything.*

Instead it felt as though the entire world constricted him.

All the sounds he thought hadn't been there evaporated. The breezes he'd barely been able to feel died and went away. He couldn't hear, smell, or taste. The city looked the same, but only because everything in it hadn't been moving before. He gazed at the knife in his left hand. It looked normal, but felt heavier.

It wasn't until he looked to the sky, in which a black bird hung frozen in the air, he realized the band was working. He stared at the bird, and over the next minute watched it flap its wings *once*.

Ok. Have to move. Before I get tired.

He ran twenty steps toward the alley the bot had taken the dummy into. At the alley's entrance, he peeked around the corner. Shadows clung to the polished path. The dark, narrow gap between monolithic towers swallowed almost all the light. A few particulates of dust hung suspended in the air.

But otherwise nothing.

He cut into the alley. He'd found a good sense of balance since being un-jacked, but he was glad for the bracer's power, else anyone watching would've seen how clumsy he was. He felt as though he were sprinting through cold broth, and he understood what Absinthe had meant.

I'll get tired.

At the alley's end he tapped the band with two fingers. The sensations of the world crashed over him, all the little feelings he'd taken for granted hitting him from every angle.

A siren shattered the morning's quiet.

"Failure! Restart!"

Lurking in the gloom across the street, the *Out* dummy stared at him.

Damnit.

He waited for the bot to emerge and steal the dummy away. He felt heat in his chest and a lump in his throat. He'd never experienced either before. He remembered the Berlitz rules, and the human emotion known as shame.

Never been stupid before, he thought.
What's that other rule?
First time for everything.

When the bot vanished into another alley and the clang of its metal legs against the street dwindled, he counted to ten beneath his breath. He shut his eyes, raised his wrist, and tapped the bracer nine times.

The world closed in on him. His senses compressed into the small space of *me*. He realized it was like living in yet another world.

First the ether.
Then the real world.
Now this.

Squeezing the knife, he ran across the street and hid in the shadow of a two-hundred story tower. He didn't know what time of day it was, but the sun's light seemed thicker than before. *Almost tangible*, he thought. *A few more taps, and I could touch the stuff.*

He stopped daydreaming. Deciding that stealth didn't matter when he was moving with the bracer activated, he jogged past several alleys. He flicked a glance into each one, and saw no dummies. In one, a scrawny creature stood frozen, its tail erect, all four of its paws off the ground. *A cat*, he remembered from a lesson learned in the ether.

In another alley, he saw a hunk of metal sitting on the polished street.

I've got an idea.

Still moving fast, he walked up to the metal. It looked weird in the gloom, heavy and orange. It was roughly the size of his leg, long and thick and rusted. He laid down his knife. After a breath, he picked the metal chunk up with a grunt, hoisted it over his head, and hurled it into the air.

As it flew, fast and high, he quickly double-tapped the band.

The crush of relativity fled again. His head felt thick, his muscles limp. Even so, he focused long enough to watch as the metal lump moved with the momentum it had earned from his almost-light-speed throw. It careened down the alley at an impossible rate, bouncing thrice off the tower walls in the blink of an eye. When it finally stopped well out of his sights on the street beyond, it made an awful racket.

It remembered. He smiled. *It remembered its momentum!*

If I threw a stone while going fast, it'd punch a hole through ten men.

And this dagger. He plucked the blade off the ground. *Absinthe was right. It'll go at my speed.*

The Outs. They'll never feel a thing.

And then he turned around. In the alley opposite his, he saw a dummy's red eyes glaring.

"Failure!"

"Restart!"

He took Absinthe's test twenty-three times that day.

He got good at starting, stopping, and slowing time.

He learned to manipulate objects he found. He tossed stones at slow speed, tapped his band, and caught them before they landed. In one alley he found a crate. He threw it straight up into the air, tapped the band four times quickly, and used a pipe to crush the crate into a hundred pieces before it hit the ground.

He learned how to conserve his energy by not tapping the band too many times. He chased animals, catching them easily, but never once daring to touch the poor, terrified things. He found sticks, rocks, old bot pieces, and several things he had no idea what to call.

Absinthe put these things in the city for me to find, he realized. *The metal chunk. The pipe. The stones. The cats.*

This city's too clean. She put them here. For me to use. To learn with.

He learned many things before the sun slipped away and the day began to die.

He became comfortable with the bracer and familiar with the sickening feeling of turning it off.

But he never passed the test.

Not even once.

And he knew Absinthe meant it to be so.

Breaking Something Beautiful

Fully dressed in a matte black grav-suit, Moz stood beside Frigg in a round chamber somewhere in the Achilles' bowels.

He felt himself sweating.

Yeori was there, too. The old man, pale as his granddaughter and smiling like one of Jupiter's crescent moons, crossed his arms and chuffed.

"Scared, Mozelle?"

Yeori was tiny next to Moz, no taller than Anjel and not much heavier, but Moz admitted the old man made him nervous.

Not even showing off his grav-suit today.
Crusty old bastard.

"I'll be fine," he muttered.

"The hell you will," countered Yeori. "You still think this'll be fun, don't you? Bodies lyin' all around you, rubble and dust and broken bots. Easy in the simulations, right? Well, let me tell you, you big lunk; ain't nuthin like breaking a city. Don't matter if it's full of *Ins*. Don't matter you weighin' ten kilos or ten thousand. It's the brain that gets bruised. You just wait and see."

"I know." He shrugged. "You've told me."

Yeori narrowed his eyes. "You *know*, do you? I guess we'll see. Hope you said your goodbyes to my Anjel. Might be you come back in a bag. Might be you don't come back at all."

Frigg glared at Yeori, and though the old man scowled, he finally shut up.

Does he hate me because I'm with Anjel? Moz wondered. *Or is he just telling it like it is?*

Doesn't matter.

I'm coming back.

He didn't have time to think on it much longer. Frigg walked up to the room's curved, chrome wall, flexed his huge fingers, and keyed a code into the wall-pad only he and a few others knew. The wall, seamless a few seconds ago, split in the middle and slid apart.

It had been one thing for Moz to daydream what the Door Chamber looked like.

It was another to see it in the flesh.

Beyond the aperture in the wall lay a vast spherical room, and a plank one-man wide spearing out to its center. Moz had expected machines, hardware and antennae protruding from every angle. But the Door Chamber, second hugest of all the rooms in the Achilles, looked empty. Save for the chrome plank dead-ending in the sphere's center, *there's nothing.*

He took two steps closer. Frigg faced him.

"The city you're going to, Moz, it's no small thing. When you switch your suit on, for a while you might feel you need to destroy everything. *Don't.* Follow your sensors' hums, find the server towers, and smash them. If the server we're looking for is there…and it might not be…find it. It *might* be mobile. It *might* be underground. It *might* be hidden in the smallest little metal house on the island. We just don't know. So anything that makes your sensors hum, you crush. Don't worry about killing *Ins*. It'll only slow you down."

"Ach," grumped Yeori. "Let him smash a few towers. Just for fun. Might be he learns something."

"No." Frigg shook his head. "The time for killing will come soon enough."

While the men bickered, Moz walked up to the plank. The silver slab stretched out into nothing, terminating in the dark, dead space in the Door Chamber's heart. He knew what this place was, but had never seen it before.

"How does the Door work?" He shivered.

"Hrmpf," scoffed Yeori.

"It's nothing spectacular," said Frigg. "You'd probably expect a hole in space-time to make an awful noise, right? Or for the Achilles to shake itself half to pieces every time we open it. It'll disappoint you. Our brothers and sisters back on Earth…they made the Door *silent*."

"Else the *Ins* would hear it opening," he guessed.

"Something like that," said Frigg.

With a shared nod, Frigg and Yeori produced identical silver-black remotes from their pockets. The little remotes had only two buttons each: one red, one black. Moz opened his mouth to ask a question, but Frigg beat him to it.

"Red opens the Door. Black closes it," said the big man. "When you're ready to come back, you tap the node on your belt. It'll take about thirty-five minutes for us to get the signal. Now, and this is important; the Door will only open in the cave, and only with the Achilles' permission. Calling for it anywhere else…pointless."

"The cave. The Krubera," he remembered.

"Right. Where our brothers and sisters await you."

"And they'll jump me to the island."

"Right again," said Frigg. "The Hatten, they call it. Some of the tallest *In* towers in the world are there. Kosi and Zamo have already gone through and jumped to cities elsewhere. They're a distraction, Moz. The Hatten, it's our real target. Full of servers, packed nice and tight. Like Yeo would say, 'Might be you can win the war *tonight*.'"

"And the *Ins* won't be waiting for me?"

Frigg frowned. "Oh, they'll have bots there. And turrets. You'll have about a half-hour before they fly in the heavy stuff. They don't know how to jump yet, so they'll come at you old-fashioned. Planes, missiles, flechettes, quake bombs. Turn your kilos way up. Let out some gravity if something comes too close. Get in. Smash some servers. Get out. And always remember where your jump-pad is"

"What's it like to jump?" He had to know.

Frigg didn't answer.

Yeori just smiled.

"It's time, Moz." Frigg tapped the remote's red button.

"See you in a few." Yeori tapped his.

Silent, black, and spherical, the Door opened. It popped into existence at the plank's end, floating in the void, a seam in space-time connected to a hole more than nine-hundred million kilometers away. He'd thought to see something bigger, but the Door hung there like an ebony bubble, its diameter barely wider than he was tall.

"So small." His mouth hung open. "And so dark."

"You're looking at Earth," said Frigg. "The Door is way down at the bottom of Krubera. It's so deep there used to be water there, but our brothers and sisters grav'd it away. It's almost a half-kilo down in the rock. It'll be dark when you go through, but friends will be waiting for you. They'll turn the lights up once you're through."

"And there'll be no time for talk, Mozelle," Yeori grunted. "Just get on the pad and jump."

"And don't die," said Frigg.

The last thing he thought of before walking down the plank and into the Door was Anjel. He imagined her sitting on his bed, her white gown resting on her pale shoulders. She had done just that when he'd left her that morning. She'd looked miserable. He hoped it was just her worrying for him, but he knew better.

She hates that I'm doing this, he thought.

She hates violence.

She's nothing like her grandfather.

He stepped into the sphere of darkness. *No rush of air*, he thought. *No noise. No slide through space-time.*

What is this thing?

Three steps deep, he felt a chill and tasted humid air. Earth's gravity, far less than the Achilles', made him feel as though he were floating. He stretched out his hands, groping his way into darkness.

He heard voices, some in the language he knew, others not.

Two glowing lamps flickered on, one to each side.

Earth.

Too easy to get here.

He made fists out of his fingers. He resisted the urge to cry out, 'one-thousand!' and increase his mass eight-fold. *To protect me…in case the Ins are here.*

"Mozelle?" creaked an old woman standing in the sad yellow light.

He looked at her, and then at the dozen men and women huddled in the shadows of a deep, damp cave. He'd never seen anything like them. They were small, not just due to Earth's weak gravity, *but because they're malnourished.* The youngest of them looked fifty years-old, and the tallest stood a full head shorter than him. Some were like him: deep-hued, their skin the color of Jupiter's darkest clouds. Others were pale as Yeori, their flesh powdery white and wrinkled.

"I'm Moz," he said with a forced smile. "Is this the Krubera?"

They came to him, hands extended, touching the matte skin of his grav-suit. He heard some of what they murmured: "Warrior," they said. "Jupiter-born. Big, even for the Achilles." He let them paw at him, feeling at once powerful and uneasy. He remembered what Frigg had taught him, that these people had lived generations in and around the Krubera, stealing from the *Ins* whenever they could, plotting the Door's creation over the span of centuries.

Scientists aboard the Achilles had been clad in pale jackets, clean and sharp as knives.

But these people.

From Earth.

The way we used to be.

The old woman came to him. She smiled, and her wrinkles made more lines on her face than ever he'd seen on Yeori's.

"Are you ready?" she asked him.

I don't know. Am I? he almost answered.

"I am," he said.

She took his huge hand into two of her tiny ones. Despite the low gravity and her advanced age, her grip felt strong. "Someday, Moz, we'll all sit down and sup together. I understand on the Achilles you eat your meals alone. But here on Earth it's traditional to eat all as one."

"Is this really Earth?" he said. "I feel…strange. The air…it tastes…better."

She smiled again. But instead of answering, she tugged him away from the darkness at his back. He glanced over his shoulder, but the Door was already gone.

Like it had never been there.

With a shiver, he followed her through the shadows. The mass of elderly parted, and the nameless crone guided him past the glowing lamps and into a corridor beyond. He'd lived on the Achilles all his life. He was accustomed to gazing out his windows into the blackness of space. But in the sumps of Krubera, the darkness felt heavy. No stars pricked the bottomless night. No reflections of Jupiter or its moons peered through the void at him.

"Only place darker…" murmured the old woman as she walked, "…is the ocean's bottom. Hard to do science down here, but this is the way of it."

He wound his way after her. Tiny glow lamps embedded in the stone lit the way. He squeezed through crevices, walked through corridors whose walls wept mineral water, and ascended steep passages hollowed out centuries ago by machines whose names he'd never know. Every so often, he glimpsed rooms off the main path. The lights from therein were silver blue, pale and beautiful, but the old woman never stopped long enough to let him take it all in.

She led him to a lift station. He looked up the hollow shaft and shuddered. And then he looked down, where a deep, dark abyss spiraled down into forever.

"The Door's machinery," said the old woman. "It's down there. Someday maybe you'll see it. Not today. Today we're going up."

He wanted to ask questions. He needed to know how they survived down here, what they did for food, and how they managed not to go mad with the darkness.

He said nothing.

He just wanted to see the one thing Frigg and Yeori had told him about.

The Sun.

The lift arrived. He stepped onto the ancient-looking thing, stood close to the old woman, and held his breath as the machine shot him and her up at a nauseating speed.

At least it's not too loud.

I want to puke.

He rode two more lifts after the first. Finally, after the third, he stepped off into a corridor bigger than anything he'd seen. A tunnel, wormed into the stone by some vast and terrible machine, opened up before him. Lights from rooms hollowed out of the walls peered down at him. Glow lamps dotted the tunnel up and down, and people stopped what they were doing to stare at him.

Is this what a city looks like?

Is this really Earth?

The tunnel bottom was its only flat part. The old woman commandeered a wheel-driven cart and gestured wordlessly for him to get on. She hit a switch. As she and he zoomed down the tunnel, he looked at all the lights dotting the walls.

Hundreds of rooms, he thought at first.

No. Thousands.

And then, after enduring countless stares and too much silence, the old woman stopped the cart. Another lift shaft lay open before him. He looked into it, and he saw light shining down from above.

"Yes. That's it," said the old woman. "The real thing. *Sunlight.*"

"It's up this lift?" he asked.

"Yes. It's just now mid-morning."

"Mid-*what*?"

"Oh, you poor dear." She patted his arm. "I'm sorry. I forgot you don't have mornings where you're from. I forgot you're new."

She opened the elevator gate. He looked behind him and saw that dozens of men and women were staring at him. Their shadows stretched along the tunnel. They stood with glow lamps in their grasps, halting their work to see him rise into the sunlight. Frigg had told him people would want to see him, but now that it was happening, he didn't know what he felt.

Pride is ugly, he remembered something Anjel had said.

Don't soak it up.

He walked onto the lift. It was larger than the last, big enough to lift a hundred people at once. He peered up, hoping to see the sun shining above, but instead he saw only reflections, pools of yellow light gleaming against dark stone.

"You'll want these," said the old woman. She handed him a pair of glasses with shadowed lenses. He'd never seen such a thing. He put them on, and all the light in the world dimmed.

"What are these called? Why do I need them?"

"Sunglasses." The old woman slipped on her own pair. "Yours are special. They won't break unless you turn your suit's kilos way up."

"But why—"

"Shhhh. You'll see."

In the next moment, he understood. The elevator rose, breaching the Krubera's rim, and a realm of light consumed him. On the Achilles, it had never been truly dark. Pale illumination was everywhere, lighting the ship's halls, bedchambers, and vast chambers of gathering.

But this was different. Nothing could have prepared him to see Earth's sky.

When the elevator stopped, he stepped off and staggered to a halt. He looked for walls, but found none. He expected ceilings, and yet the heavens went on forever. Pale clouds drifted across a serene blue canvas. Light came from all directions, almost blinding even through his glasses, *and so, so warm*.

The first time he glimpsed the sun, it was in a pool of water at his feet. White and golden, ten times more powerful than anything he'd seen from the

Achilles' windows, its reflection watched him in the water.

"Rain's just passed," said the old woman. "Come this way. Jump pad's just around that hill."

She walked ahead. He wandered in a stupor behind her. He looked up again, and finally saw the true sun. A cloud had just scudded by, but once it cleared, he felt the warmth washing over him. He wished he could tear his grav-suit off, that he might feel the light touch his skin.

He followed the woman, never once tearing his gaze from the sky. If the Achilles was his home, his small and sacred temple, the skies above Krubera were a cathedral without end.

And the sun, he thought. *It's like Anjel. It's...beautiful.*

He rounded a rocky hill, heedless of all other things, until the old woman snared his arm and directed him into the shadows at the hill's far side.

"I'm sorry, Moz," she said. "No time to take it all in. You're going to jump now. You won't like the feeling; no one does. We'll send you, then we'll jump a spare pad right after you. Same spot."

He snapped back to the here and now. "How long will it take?"

"About twenty minutes. The Hatten's thousands of kilometers away from here. You'll go up...and then you'll come down. Did Frigg configure your suit?"

"You mean the repulsors? So I won't hit the ground too hard and make a crater?"

"Yes." She frowned. "Those."

He nodded. The old woman lifted a grey canvas attached to the hillside. Behind it lay the jump pad. It wasn't anything like he expected. He'd thought to see some grand device, a trampoline for rocketing humans across the globe. But the real jump pad was just six metal bars with a membrane stretched taut between them. He didn't know how it would work. He didn't believe it.

"So…now what?"

The old woman took the pad down and laid it across the ground. It must not have weighed much; she didn't even strain to move it. As she knelt and pried open a thin panel on one of the bars, he crossed his arms and doubted.

"How's it work?"

"I give it coordinates. I tell it to drop you on a street in the Hatten instead of on a roof or in the water. When I'm done, you stand on it. And then you fly."

"How come we don't just send bombs? Or missiles? You know…to destroy the whole city. Or *all* the *In* cities, for that matter."

She peered up at him. It was obvious she'd been asked the same question before. "We're not like the *Ins*, Moz. We don't want genocide."

"But Yeori—"

"It's programmed." She stood up and backed away. She kept looking up to the sky, *like she thinks someone's watching us.*

"So I just stand on it?"

"Yes." She pointed. "Right there. In the middle. Set your kilos to one-thousand. Else the g's will pull you to pieces."

He gulped, blinked, and looked at the sun once more. Closing his eyes, he activated his grav-suit. "One-thousand," he said in a monotone voice.

Just watch, he thought.

Damn jump pad's gonna break.

The pad didn't break. Its membrane didn't even sink. When he activated the suit, he didn't feel any different, though he did see the old woman almost fall over. And the water in a nearby puddle ripple and rise. And two pebbles on the ground tumble slowly toward him. The suit made him many times more massive than before. His gravity increased sevenfold, wanting to pull everything closer.

"Take a deep breath," he heard her say. The suit's mass field distorted her voice, but he understood all the same. "And pray your repulsors work," she added while backing away.

He didn't take the breath fast enough. The old woman shouted, "Jump!" and the pad shot him into the sky. He didn't feel himself accelerate. He was simply stationary in one moment, and then flying at thousands of kilometers per hour. The Krubera dwindled beneath him. His arms were pinned to his sides, his suit rippling, and the clouds rushing toward him.

He felt terrified.

And exhilarated.

She was right, he managed to think as he tore into heaven.

Without the suit, I'd be torn to shreds.

He shot through the clouds and into the deep blue above. He felt the cold seep into his suit, working its way down to his skin. Frigg had told him the suit's gravity field would keep him alive while jumping, but a part of him was still afraid. *What if I use up all the air trapped in the field?* he thought. *What if the old woman miscalculated and shot me too high?*

I'll turn to ice.

I'll shatter on the streets.

Higher and higher he soared. The minutes felt like hours, and his breaths the same as waves crashing against him. When he reached his zenith, he saw Earth far below him, as alien as any world, and he saw the void above, littered with silver satellites and black-chrome defense batteries. He remembered something Frigg had said: 'The *Ins* have all their weapons pointed outward. They thought we'd build ships and missiles to conquer Earth from the sky.'

'But they never dreamed we'd come from *within*.'

He began his descent. He worried about freezing in the upper atmosphere, but as the friction built against his suit's grav-field, flames erupted a finger's width from his face. The beautiful sky-blues vanished behind a blizzard of reds and oranges. *If the suit fails*, he thought, *I die.*

He felt himself falling. He wished he could see. *The sky. The ground. Anything.* He was glad Frigg had told him not to eat, else he'd have retched. *And my gravity would've made it all stick to my face.* The repulsors on his suit kicked in, and he was sure the deceleration would peel back his skin and spread his bones like sticks into the wind. But it didn't. Nine-hundred years of living on the Achilles had served his people well. They'd defeated Jupiter's gravity. One man falling was far easier.

The darkness above burned away. The ground rushed toward him, a blur of greens, browns, and silvers flashing just beyond the flames still roiling against his suit. He felt stretched, pulled as thin as the hairs on Yeori's head.

And then he hit the ground.

Where he landed, the street cracked and black powder filled the air. A plume of dust erupted, then dispersed. He'd seen the pictures of the cities Frigg had showed him, but when the powder thinned and he saw endless towers surrounding him on all sides, he felt tiny. Thousands of silver spires pierced the heavens, which weren't blue as they'd been over the Krubera, but grey and sickly. He didn't know what the clouds meant. He assumed the worst.

What'd Yeori say?

Start at three-thousand kilos.

More than twenty-one times denser.

He opened his mouth to activate his suit again, but heard a clatter behind him. Just as promised, the old woman had jumped a second pad to him, already programmed for a return trip to the Krubera. It landed on the street behind him. It had repulsors, but not enough to keep it from skipping along the street and clattering upside-down against a tower.

Remember where this is, he told himself.

Hope the fall didn't break it.

All the things Frigg had told him caught fire in his mind. He'd thought he'd been ready, but it turned out Yeori was right. He was confused, nervous, and unsure of how to start. Any moment, bots would start pouring out of the towers. He'd either pull it together, *or die.*

To calm himself, he thought of Anjel. She'd kissed him only yesterday, but her kiss hadn't been like the hundreds of others she'd given him. She'd clasped his face in her little hands and told him, 'Come back, Moz. Please. I love you.'

Figure it out, he thought.

Survive.

"Three-thousand!" he said out loud.

His suit made no sound. It didn't matter. He knew it'd worked. The last granules of street powder floating in the air curled and came toward him. In moments, he reckoned himself a miniature Saturn, the dust swirling in rings around him. He took two steps, and felt powerful when the street cracked beneath his feet.

Yeori said he did eleven-thousand.

...wonder what it feels like.

The sensors responsible for finding *In* servers hummed beneath his suit and against his chest. One server was already near. He ran down the street, leaving broken stones and grey clouds in his wake. The sensor tugged him down one alley and onto an adjacent street. He stopped in the middle of a thoroughfare overlooked by towers two-hundred stories high. He expected bots to burst out of hiding and unload tens of thousands of flechettes at him, but nothing came.

His sensor hummed hot against his skin. It guided him back and to his right. He ran thirty steps, pulverizing the street, and stopped before a tower even taller than the others.

It was huge. *Three-hundred stories high.* Its windowless, chrome-silver walls wore the shadows of all the towers standing near. Its doors were sealed, visible only by black lines.

'The doors are only for bots,' he remembered Frigg saying.

'Damn *Ins* don't need 'em,' Yeori had added. 'Fucking dreamers never come out.'

He stood before the tower, his sensor buzzing so hard it hurt. He looked up, squinting even in the gloom, wincing from the magnitude of steel and chrome. He wondered how the *Ins* had built such a thing while sleeping. He wondered what this place had looked like before the towers had gone up.

His bravado evaporated.

He didn't feel big anymore.

"Six-thousand," he uttered.

To pack six-thousand kilos into the size of one man was no mild thing. His gravity sucked up bits of broken street, which clung to his legs as if glued on. His rings of dust flew faster, colliding against the tower in a hail of sparks. He felt inhuman, a singularity, a mobile black hole denser than the Earth's core.

The server's in there. He regarded the tower.

And so are thousands of people.

He walked within reach of the tower. At his mass and density, even if the whole tower came crashing down on him, it was unlikely to injure him.

"Seven-thousand."

Just to be sure.

He reached back to punch the door. To begin destroying the tower. *To bring it down.*

But before he struck, something tickled his back.

He spun around. Two bots had emerged from the towers behind him and were emptying caches of flechettes at him. The little needles came at him by the thousand, whining and tearing through his dust rings, exploding against his suit. He flinched and raised his arm, but it was needless. At his density, the flechettes hit him and flattened. Some of them shattered and joined his dust rings. Others stuck to him, a second skin of steel overlaying his grav-suit.

None of them hurt.

He picked up a chunk of street and hurled it at one of the bots. At one-hundred fifty kilometers per hour, the stone brick hit the bot in its big round bottom. Sparks erupted from punctured steel. The bot collapsed in a heap, its death rattle cracking the midday gloom. He almost felt sad for it.

The other bot looked on with three antennae eyes, seeming to recognize what had happened.

Moz charged it.

He considered calling out, "One-hundred!" to release the gravity stored in his suit. The shockwave would have crushed the bot and rattled every tower within a kilometer, but he decided not to risk death just yet.

Only in dire need, Frigg said.
And never in close quarters.

The bot's flechettes ran out just before he got to it. A panel flipped open on its flank, revealing a lance for emitting quake bombs, but he ripped the lance's tip off, shattered the bot's three eyes with a backhand, and with three quick punches reduced his mechanized foe to a pile of scrap steel and sparking wires.

With little effort, he hurled the broken machine down the street. It landed a quarter-kilometer away, where it collapsed with a ruinous rattle and a plume of black smoke.

He faced the tower.

They're trying to kill me.

Yeori was right.

"Eight-thousand."

He sprinted at the tower.

And went right through it.

He perforated the outer wall. It tore like paper. Inside the tower's bottom floor, he collided with steel columns, glass elevator shafts, and rooms barred with silver doors. Through all of these he ran, smashing everything, less afraid with each breath. Nothing could stop him. He was a missile, an engine of death. It was just like Yeori had boasted. 'You'll feel invincible, Moz,' the old man had said.

'You'll like it.'

In a storm of fists and shoulders, he swam through the tower's heart and emerged on its other side. A grey cloud of glass and powdered steel trailed him onto the smooth, black street beyond. He backed away from the tower he'd gutted. The silver spire quivered. The street fractured. He wondered if he'd have to charge through again, but thought better of it. Support beams inside the tower shuddered and cracked. Hard black lines crawled up the outer walls, snaking through chrome as everything fell apart.

Better run. Don't care what Yeo said. Don't want that on top of me.

He sprinted away while looking over his shoulder. He heard a sound like the world cracking in two, but felt only the mildest vibration in his feet. When the tower collapsed, it came down in a torrent of ruined silver and glass. First the outer walls sheared off and spilled onto the street. Then the insides crumbled, a hail of metallic slabs tumbling at the same rate as the storm of shattered glass and pulverized machinery.

He saw *Ins* falling. Cables snaked from their necks, arms, and chests. They looked asleep.

But they still looked human.

No.

Wait.

This isn't right.

His sensors stopped buzzing. The tower's server was destroyed. He barely noticed. As the spire collapsed, a black plume devoured the street. Particulates spiraled around him, clinging to his gravity, a million tiny moons wanting to collide with him. He saw pale flashes in the great black storm.

The last of the Ins falling.

With one tower's fall, the next nearest began to crumble. He gulped when he glimpsed it through the roiling smoke. He felt sick when he saw silver shards peel off its flanks and spear the street far below. He heard thunder from the first tower's death. He saw oceans of shadows, showers of skin.

Anjel can never know. He backed away.

She won't love me after this.

He might've watched the towers fall to the very last speck of dust, but a glint of something black and shining caught his awareness. He peered to the sky and saw two bots whirring above the street. The panels on their sides were open.

Quake bombs.

Each bot ejected a bomb at him. He couldn't hear them over the collapsing towers, but he knew what they were. *Bright red. Little bouncy balloons. Full of death.* He forgot his fear. He sprinted three steps and jumped as high as he could.

And as he rose, he cried out, "One hundred!"

Instantly, his suit's gravity expelled itself. Seven-thousand nine-hundred kilos of pent-up force struck every surface on the street. Thrown off-target, the quake bombs hit other towers. The bots fractured and spun to their deaths. With the loss in mass, he expected his momentum to carry him up and into the sky, but instead he came down hard and fast. His knees hit the shattered street. He rolled through the rubble, dazed and bleeding, as the smoke from falling towers consumed him.

Ouch.

Quake bombs.

Would've leveled those towers no matter where they hit.

The bots...

They don't care how many they kill.

He staggered to his feet. His lungs burned and his bones hurt. As he stood, a fine glass shower falling on him, he realized he'd made a crater when he'd released his mass.

Two stories below street level.

And still alive.

Bigger shards of glass and steel fragments fell all around. He waited another two breaths and grunted, "Six-thousand." The ruinous rain stopped hurting, though not his insides.

He climbed out of the crater. Chunks of street broke off beneath his hands. Somewhere in the smoke, he heard still another tower crumbling, already the fifth to fall. He heard fresh bots whirring and felt flechettes singing against his skin.

He ran.

The city seemed a maze of smoke and steel. The jump pad was two streets away, lying against a tower that looked exactly the same as the others. He sprinted down an alley, ducking between two towers just as a trio of quake bombs hit the street behind him. The force of their impact sent him sprawling out the alley's other end, a long black rut carved out of the street he'd fallen on.

"Idiots!" he shouted as he picked himself up and ran again. "You're killing *everyone!*"

It didn't matter. The bots flew after him, ejecting flechettes and bombs indiscriminately. He supposed the only thing saving him was the thick black smoke of five, *no...seven towers* falling to their deaths and obscuring the bots' sensors. Ashes choked every alley. Steel and glass tempests made a crunching carpet for him to run on. *In* bodies, some pale as milk...*others dark as me*...lay strewn by the thousands, a vast graveyard for him to navigate.

He rounded a corner and hoped not to die. Six bots, three eyes gleaming on each, came after him. He saw his jump pad, half-buried in glass, lying against a tower.

Fake 'em out, he thought. *My only shot.*

He sprinted five steps right. The bots ejected their quake bombs. Planting his heel on the only part of the street that wasn't pulverized, he spun and went left.

One of the quake bombs bounced and hit a tower dead-center. Another pair collided in mid-air and ruptured too high to kill him. The other three hit the ground thirty steps behind him.

He went down again. At six-thousand kilos, he made another hole in the street, though this one was shallower. Even though he was denser than every surface he hit, his impact hurt like nothing he'd ever felt. Rock turned to powder beneath him. Waves of gravity from the quake bombs rolled over him, disrupting his suit, opening millisecond-long windows of vulnerability during which his bones rippled and his insides compressed.

Get. Up.

He stood. Ashes and ruin clung to him. More towers fell behind him...*and ahead.* The bots fired more flechettes. *Out of bombs*, he hoped. *Or maybe...my suit...they think it's broken.*

He ran for the jump pad. The street was in tatters, not flat enough to launch from. Without thinking, he plucked the pad up and ran straight through the tower wall. When he erupted from the other side, the smoke was gone and the bots hadn't found him yet.

He didn't think.

He didn't look to see if the tower was falling behind him.

He laid the pad down and said, "One-thousand."

And forgot everything that happened afterward.

Too Easy to Kill

Flying was nothing like Rafe had anticipated. During his years of being jacked-in, he'd soared over the planets he'd created, hovered atop imaginary clouds, and torn through deep space at impossible speeds. He'd always insisted on using real-life physics. He'd imagined jets, copters, rockets, and deep space shuttles, and he'd fashioned his *In* universe to make them all feel as if they'd been real.

But as it turned out, being strapped into a real-world jet as it speared through the stratosphere felt nothing like it had in the ether.

His chair vibrated so hard he thought his bones would shake out of his skin. His eyes, even protected by the goggles Toggle had given him, quivered in their sockets. Pilotless, the silver jet knifed through the air at more than three thousand kilometers per hour. If he didn't know better, he'd have thought Absinthe was trying to kill him.

Please land, he thought.

Please, please, please.

Oh god.

The jet lurched, the world turned sideways, and his chair shook even harder. His insides went one direction, then another. The jet had no windows, and yet somehow, with his stomach leaping into his chest, he sensed he was falling. Then slowing down. Then stopping.

The ground. He sagged in his chair. *We're near it.*

What'd Toggle call this feeling?
Nausea.

He heard Absinthe's voice in his earpiece.

"Rafe," she chirped, "unlock your seatbelt."

He didn't move. He just breathed. He swallowed the taste in his mouth, and he felt sick again.

"We don't have any time." The friendliness in her voice dried up. "Unlock your belt and go to the door."

He blinked hard and pushed the grey button on the chair's armrest. All at once, the taut silver belts sprang off his chest and waist. He'd never felt so *imprisoned* in his life. And with the belts falling off, he'd never felt as free.

"Good." Absinthe was only pretending to be patient now.

She's mad enough to slap me.
She doesn't fake nice well.

He stood up and pulled off his goggles. He felt as wobbly as he had when they'd first un-jacked him. He patted his chest and waist, and he touched the ebony bracer on his forearm.

Insides still in.
Knife on my belt.
She said this would be easy.
Yeah right.

He walked through the jet's cabin. The other seven seats were empty. They looked like no one had ever sat in them. In fact, the cabin's chrome interior looked pristine, as if nothing, not even the pilot-bot, had touched any part of it before.

At the jet's only door, he stopped. Outlined in black, the seamless chrome was all that stood between him and the rest of the world. He pressed his palm against it, and a man-sized panel slid open.

Sunlight poured into the cabin.

The Iranabian city of Yadhi sprawled beneath him.

Although Rafe had created planets, he'd never dreamed anything like Yadhi. Lying atop a vast plateau, it looked endless in every direction. In its center stood towers that would've breached the clouds had any dared to surf the perfect blue sky. Smaller towers, silver, black, and grey, lined the banks of dagger-straight canals, whose waters were as bright and clear as the heavens.

Twenty-thousand towers, at least, he guessed.
Five-thousand of us in every one.
One-hundred million.

"Wake the hell up," Absinthe snapped in his ear.

"Sorry," he blurted.

Too fast, the jet dropped below the skyline and into a crowded sea of silver knives. He lurched in the open door, clinging to two straps dangling from the cabin ceiling. He hadn't noticed it before, but smoke crawled into the sky near the tallest of the towers. He smelled something in the air. Something awful.

"What is that?" he asked Absinthe.

"The smell?" she guessed right.

"Yeah."

"Burning bodies."

He shuddered. The jet dropped down to just a meter off the ground. Above a four-street intersection, it hovered and spewed pale smoke into the air. Black chrome towers, a hundred stories high, loomed on all sides. It felt just like Alta Sur, only darker...*and hotter*.

Already he was sweating.

"Hurry," Absinthe's voice crackled in his ear, "he's destroying the biggest tower. He's going to jump away. If he escapes, you've failed."

He leapt out of the cabin and landed hard on the silver street. The jet pumped its hover pads and soared fifty stories high, where it floated utterly still, its reflection a hard white line against the towers' black sides.

In a flash, his weeks of training on the streets of Alta Sur came back to him.

Eight taps.

He drummed his fingers against the black bracer. After eight little taps, the world constricted. The jet's roar faded to nothing. The boom of distant quake bombs and falling towers fell away. He was used to the feeling, but hated it. Even on the wide-open street, the world standing still made him feel claustrophobic.

He didn't need to run. Walking would conserve stamina. Absinthe had taught him that once he'd activated his bracer, he'd last longer by treating everything like a casual stroll.

'Think of it as foreplay,' she'd told him.

'You'll like it more if you don't rush through it.'

He remembered Absinthe as he walked. It was easier to think of her than of what he was about to do. He wished he understood her. He wished he could sneak into her thoughts and unravel the secrets behind her eyes. When he'd finished his training and she'd taken him to her private chambers, he'd known what would happen. She bedded him, and she did it *hard*.

For the first time since being un-jacked, he'd felt something that reminded him of being *In*. He didn't care that she'd only made love to him as a reward for finishing his training. He only cared that he'd finally gotten something he wanted.

And for as much as he'd expected making love in real-life to be different than in the ether, it turned out it was the one thing that had felt almost the same. Absinthe had done everything he dreamed of, everything he desired. For once, she'd been yielding, just like the girls he'd chased in *In*. She'd worshipped him, all the while smirking, and he loved it.

But afterward she'd walked away without a word. As if he'd dreamed the encounter. As if she'd felt nothing.

And he was left with more questions than ever.

For a few breaths he worried that somehow Absinthe would know he was thinking about her. He walked a little faster, but soon slowed again.

She can't hear me, he remembered.

I'm going faster than everyone in the world.

He crawled out of his mind and back into Yadhi. One block away, he saw a cloud of fine black powder hanging motionless in the air. He knew what to expect. A lone *Out* marauder had been reported rampaging in the city's heart. 'The *Out* sonofabitch is tryin' to smash our servers,' Emperor had cursed. 'And he's dropping towers like dominoes.'

"What's a domino?" he'd asked as they led him to the jet.

No one had answered.

As he neared the cloud of black ash, he breathed heavier. He'd only walked three blocks, but his heart hadn't stopped thumping. Being afraid was exhausting, it turned out.

I need to hurry.

He jogged to the block's end and staggered to a stop. Of the thirty grand towers that had once stood in Yadhi's center, only three remained. The others lay in heaps of twisted, smoking steel. Bodies were tangled in the wreckage. Piles of corpses were heaped under carpets of glass. Some still burned, while others looked asleep, their *In* cables connected to *nothing.*

Mouth open, he surveyed the destruction. He saw bots with their eye-cables torn off, their hulls split open, and their legs twisted. Everywhere were quake bomb craters. He remembered the pictures Toggle had showed him. The bomb holes were shallow but wide, and the streets split open to the end of his sights. In one of the towers still standing, he saw two gaping holes, doubtless the bombs' work.

He remembered what Absinthe had told him.

"The *Out* soldier…he'll wait until the bombs are almost on him, then he'll shed his gravity. All the projectiles headed his way…they'll reverse."

"So why even bother with bombs?" he'd asked.

"Not a lot of options, Rafe." She had walked away. "We thought we'd never need these kinds of weapons again. Even so, we've killed dozens of *Outs* before, even ones with grav-suits. Sometimes all it takes is luck."

And a willingness to destroy our own cities, he thought.

He walked into the carnage. With the black bracer activated, the clouds of smoke and ash stood almost still. The deeper he wandered into the ruin of fallen towers, the slower he went. He couldn't tell if any bots were left to defend Yadhi. He didn't see any bombs in the air, or any hanging storms of flechettes.

To find the *Out* marauder, he knew what he needed to do.

He tapped the band with two fingers.

And let the world catch up to him.

All at once, the sounds, sights, and smells hit him. He heard an explosion from inside a mound of fallen steel. He felt the heat, not just from the fires, but from the sun glaring down on him. A sea of smoke blossomed just ahead, and then broke apart in the hot gale rushing through Yadhi's heart.

He did what Absinthe had told him to do. He shut his eyes and listened.

No more quake bombs going off.

No bots humming.

That tower over there…about to fall.

A steady thump.

Streets cracking.

The Out…he's walking toward the biggest tower.

He took three slow breaths and tapped the band nine times. The world felt no slower than before, but the silence felt heavier than ever. Eyes fixed straight ahead, he weaved down a ruined boulevard, stepping over holes, gliding around twisted steel columns, and pretending not to notice the bodies of men, women, and children.

He tried not to see them.

But he did.

Most of Yadhi's citizens weren't pale like him. Those whose faces he accidentally glimpsed were bronze and gold, the color of sun-touched copper. He jogged past a woman whose big eyes were open and staring at the sun, and he saw her beauty destroyed. He realized how sheltered he'd lived inside *In*. All the worlds he'd created and all the imaginary people he'd triggered to evolve had been just like him. They'd been pale. They'd been pretty. They'd been protected from diversity by his lack of experience in the real world.

He thought he'd created something beautiful and true. But his mind had been too narrow.

My experiments are ruined.
I poisoned everything.
I didn't know.

The *Out* enemy was close, he sensed. He ascended a hummock of ruined steel and clambered down to the fractured street on the other side. The only things moving were the fires, which wavered like crimson flags in an impossibly slow wind. He walked through a puddle of burning oil leaking out of a broken bot. It couldn't hurt him. The flames didn't even waver from his passing until he was twenty steps past.

Of the three grand towers left standing in Yadhi's heart, the largest of them all lay just ahead. The street he walked led straight to it, as did most of the others. Like a spider in the center of its web, the black, many-tiered fortress speared the blue sky. *Three-hundred floors,* he guessed. *The Out saved it for last.*

He saw his enemy a few hundred steps ahead. With the black bracer activated, the *Out* was frozen.

His back to me.

The *Out* was a big, dark-skinned man, bigger than any he'd ever seen. And in his grav-suit, he was surely the most powerful living thing on the planet. Everywhere he'd stomped, the street had buckled. And on both the big man's sides, clouds of black grit hovered. Rafe was glad he couldn't see his face.

Don't want to.

Too dangerous.

He gulped his breaths down. His head ached and his muscles burned. He walked a hundred steps closer, and left beads of his sweat hanging in the air after they fell out of the bracer's range.

Don't get too close, he reminded himself. *Wait for it.*

He's got to shed his gravity before he escapes. And then's my chance.

He touched the knife on his belt. The thought of plunging it into a living being didn't agree with his stomach. He'd never seen blood before today. But after a walk through three and a half blocks of Yadhi, he imagined he'd seen more than any human ever had.

He closed his eyes and remembered what Absinthe had said:

"When you get near him, find a place to hide. Wait until he expels his mass, then freeze the world and kill him."

Fifty steps away from the *Out*, he knelt to the street. He needed to think, to catch his breath. *If I wait, he'll destroy that tower. Thousands more will die. Killing him will be easy, but...*

He picked up a chunk of broken street from a tomb of rubble. It was the same size as his fist, and as hard as steel.

Bombs won't hurt him.

Nor will flechettes.

But a rock going at a few thousand kilometers per hour.

Why didn't I think of it sooner?

He did the math in his head. *It'd be just like in Alta Sur*, he reckoned. *Just like the pebbles I threw. The ones that punched holes in that tower.* With the bracer powered up, the world and everything in it believed he was going at near-light speed. It wouldn't matter how dense or how massive the *Out* was.

I can save everyone in the tower.

Somehow he wasn't sure if it would work. He looked at the rock in his hand, squeezed it, and ambled closer to the *Out* marauder. The big man had moved a few inches while Rafe had been thinking.

A minute for me.

A tenth of a second for him.

This'll work.

He hurled the chunk of street at the *Out*.

And missed him by two meters.

Feeling stupid, he wiped another cloud of sweat from his forehead. He was exhausted now. His eyelids felt like iron curtains. His fingers were numb.

But even so.

He picked up another chunk of street. This one was smaller, only half the size of the other. Still a good thirty steps from the *Out*, he threw the rock. When it left his hand, it didn't slow down. Gravity didn't bend it. *It has escape velocity*, he knew right away. *It'd make orbit.*

It flew in an unimaginably straight line. And when it hit the big man in the left shoulder, the *Out*'s ten-thousand kilos didn't matter. The rock exploded, but did its damage. Rafe saw the shockwave spreading out in slow-motion.

Shit! He panicked. *Right at me!*

He dropped to the ground, covered his head with his hands, and waited. Had he looked up, he'd have seen the sphere of dust blow by. He'd have watched a nearby girder topple. And had he been standing, he'd have had a thousand tiny holes in him from the rock's fragments.

He was lucky.

When he finally clambered back to his feet, he winched. His calf leaked blood in three small places, but nothing worse. Almost everything in the world looked dead.

Including the *Out*.

The big man was down. The rock hadn't punched through him, but the shockwave had knocked him flat. Gasping for breath, Rafe staggered over to him and double-tapped the ebony band. The world caught up to him again. He heard the last bits of rock and dust falling a half-block away. He swore he felt the ground subtly shake, but couldn't tell whether it was real...*or whether I'm about to black out.*

He went to his knees beside the *Out*. If somehow the big man were still alive, *he could reach up and snap me in two.* He looked into the *Out*'s wide-open eyes. Blood pooled beneath the big man's mouth. His grav-suit was intact, but the shape of the *Out*'s arm and spine suggested that everything beneath was broken. Or turned to jelly.

The *Out* was dead.

On his arm Rafe saw a name imprinted.

Zamo.

Rafe retched. He hadn't felt this sick since his first days after being un-jacked. After emptying his guts on the street, he looked up to the huge black tower and shook his head at it. "Saved you all," he muttered out loud. "If Absinthe and Togs had it their way, I'd have let you all die. What a mess that would've been, right?"

Delirious, he sank to his bottom beside the fallen *Out*. He looked at the big man's eyes. "You don't look all that evil," he said. "Just big. *Really* big. How'd you get so big anyway? And why?" He looked to the ruined towers, the sea of dead *Ins*, and the vast clouds of smoke. "Why couldn't you just have stayed out there? *Out* in space…or wherever you're from. Why?"

The *Out* never answered. The next thing Rafe heard was the jet soaring overhead. It sank down to the street, where it hovered a few meters above a graveyard of stone and steel.

"What happened?" Absinthe chirped in his ear. He realized that in her perception, he'd only been on the ground for less than a minute.

"I got him," he murmured.

"Look at him," she said. "So I can see him, too."

He stood up and looked down at the dead *Out*. Hating the sight, he quickly looked away.

"Fucking hell, Rafe," she snapped. "Those aren't knife wounds. What'd you do to him?"

"A rock." He staggered toward the jet.

"A rock?"

"In the shoulder. While at nine taps."

"Did he expel his gravity?" She sounded agitated.

"No. Didn't matter. Rock exploded. I think I've got some in my leg."

He reached the jet. A silver stair lowered itself, and he climbed aboard. A half-minute later, after he'd strapped himself in and sank into the chair, he heard Absinthe's breath in his earpiece again. He knew she'd been waiting for him to sit.

"It was nice what you did," she said. "Good thinking…the rock. But there's just one little problem."

"Problem? I don't know what you mean."

"Of course you don't," she hissed. "How could you? You didn't wait for him to shed his gravity, Rafe. His suit's still on. That's ten-thousand kilos of man lying dead on the street. No one can clean him up, not without dying. Not today. Not tomorrow. Not until a few hundred years from now, when that damn suit finally forgets to be heavy."

He put his head back and shut his eyes. He felt the jet rise and tear off into the sky, only this time he didn't care. "A hundred thousand people just died," he said. "and you're worried about cleaning up one *Out*?"

He heard silence. After a while, he thought maybe she'd let him be. Then finally his earpiece crackled. She was back, and she was calmer than before.

"You know what?" she said. "You're right, Rafe. It's just one little *Out*. One down. Three to go. You get back here. We'll patch you up. And we'll send you out for the others."

He fell silent for a second, then blurted, "I thought you said three *Outs*? As in three total? But I killed one, so now there should only be two."

"Sorry, Rafe." She didn't sound sorry at all. "That's the tough part about reality. Things change out here.

"And when things change, *you* have to change right along with them."

Guardian Anjel

"**S**even broken ribs. Fractured jaw. Three broken fingers. Dislocated shoulder. Popped kidney. Little aneurysms all over the place. And three tiny flechettes in your leg…not even sure how those got in there."

Moz cracked his eyes open long enough to look at the medic. The cold blue lights were too bright, even for the Achilles. He let his eyelids slam shut. And he listened.

"Will he make it?" he heard Yeori rasp.

"Of course he will," uttered a woman. He felt her fingers squeeze on his forearm, and he knew it was Anjel.

"It's funny," said the medic. "We've mastered gravity. We've poked holes in deep space. But the human body is still what confounds us. It's more complicated inside one of us than the whole rest of the universe."

"Yes, yes," Yeori grunted. "But will he make it?"

Moz knew the medic without looking. The tall, wire-thin pale man was as cantankerous as Yeori, and only half as old. And so, when the medic declared, "Moz ain't dying on *my* watch," he smirked and let himself go back to sleep.

* * *

Later, much later, he awoke. The blue lights were dim. The medics and Yeori were gone.

And I'm still in the med-ward.

"Moz?" Anjel must have been sleeping, too. Her voice sounded fragile.

"I'm here." He opened his eyes. The blue lights didn't hurt anymore, and the silence beyond Anjel was absolute.

"Oh thank god, Moz." She scooted closer on her stool. She looked exhausted, her white hair a glorious tangle.

The most beautiful creature alive.

"How'd I get back?" he asked.

"You jumped. Your suit still worked. Long enough that you didn't hit the ground and make a crater, anyway. It's fried now, of course."

"They making me a new one?"

"They'd better not be." She squeezed his wrist harder than before.

He closed his eyes to think. His head still hurt, and he hadn't yet worked up the courage to move his arms and legs. *To see if they're still attached.*

"Anjel?"

"Yes?"

"I had a thought."

"That's a first," she laughed, though he knew tears were sliding down her cheeks.

"How come the *Ins* didn't use my jump-pad?"

"What do you mean?"

"I left it behind. You know…when I jumped back to the Krubera. At least, I think I did. I really don't remember."

"Yeo says it's something about the weight." She petted his forehead. "Not sure exactly. Whatever's jumping has to be a thousand kilos, I think. Else it won't work. I heard someone say they tried to shoot bombs at the Krubera using pads before. But they blew up. Along with the pad. Wrong weight or something."

"Oh."

She touched his cheek. He raised his arm to hold her hand. *Still got one arm.* He smiled. *Even if it's full of IVs.* While staring into her green eyes, he fell in love all over again. Earth, the *Ins*, the bots, and the falling towers felt light-years away.

"How long have I been out?"

"You were still up when you landed in the Krubera," she said. "At least, that's what they say. And you were still awake when they brought you back here. They had to cut your suit off. Wasn't easy. You were a thousand kilos. They shed your gravity in the Boom Room. I felt it through two doors."

"Sorry." It hurt when he snorted.

"All that exercise...it saved you, Moz. They say anyone in lesser condition would've died. Heart would've stopped. More bones would've broken."

"Can't wait to get back at it." It hurt when he smiled. "Feelin' better already."

"Moz, it's not funny."

"I know. But I bet Kosi and Zamo would be proud. Always tried to get as big as them. Never quite got there, but survived anyway."

She looked hard at him. "Kosi and Zamo are dead."

He rolled his eyes at that. It hurt, but only a little. "Yeah, right. Those two? How many times have they gone through the Door? Twenty? Thirty?"

"I'm serious." She squeezed his arm harder than ever.

He stopped smiling. He faced her, and for the first time saw her tears. She wasn't sobbing, *just leaking*.

"What do you mean, *dead*?"

She swiped her tears away. "I mean they didn't come back from their jumps. Nothing, not even a piece of them. Our friends in the caves think the *Ins* have some kind of new weapon. Got Zamo in Yadhi, then Kosi a few days later."

Zamo? His heart beat a crushing rhythm inside him. *Kosi?*

"But that means…we've lost?"

"I don't know, Moz. I don't have the answers. Frigg says our scientists are working on a new grav system for the Achilles. It'll be strong enough to break Jupiter's hold. When it's done, we can leave the system. We can go wherever. The *Ins* won't be able to shoot missiles at us anymore. Or even find us. We'll be free."

The blood in his neck simmered. He sat up in a mess of IV cables and electrodes. His legs were still attached, his other arm, too. He didn't really care.

"We're running away?"

"I didn't say that." Anjel shook her head. She didn't look sad anymore, but *conflicted.* "Yeo and lots of the others…they want to make more suits. They want to train more of us to fight. To wreck more *In* cities. Others want to leave. But nobody wants to abandon the people in the Krubera. The *Outs*, we're all called. We're family."

"So why don't they just come through the Door?"

"They don't want to. They've got their way of life down there, mining the sump for water, farming moss and plants and whatever else for food. It's a strange life, but it's theirs. Besides, there's too many. They couldn't all fit on the Achilles. But they've sacrificed too much for us just to abandon them. They want freedom, same as us. But they want it on Earth."

He went silent for a few seconds, then looked at the ceiling. A coiled mass of cables snaked down and into the machine beside him. He felt pitiful.

"I look like an *In*," he finally murmured.

"What's that?" She hadn't heard him.

"I destroyed the server," he said. "The *In* server. The big one in the Hatten. I don't want to talk about the rest of it, but the server definitely went down. I guess it wasn't the one, huh? The important one?"

Anjel bit her lip. *Just like she does whenever she's not telling me something.*

"What is it?" he pressed.

"Nothing."

"Tell me." He snared her wrist. She was strong, thin as she was, and she pulled it free.

"Moz, it'll just frustrate you."

"So frustrate me."

She sighed. It was a beautiful noise, and with it he almost gave up asking.

No. Not this time.

"What do you know, Anjel? What did Yeo tell you?"

She looked everywhere in the room except at him. She stalled, sitting in silence for a long while.

And then she gave in.

"The server's mobile," she said.

"Of course it's mobile," he snorted. "I bet they move it from building to building all the time."

"No, I mean *mobile*. As in; it moves by itself. That's what the Krubera think. They think the pings they've been getting on the other big servers were decoys. They think the server that houses all the *Out*-hate is inside an AI – an artificial intelligence. Inside a bot, maybe. Or maybe it's in one of the satellites. Or maybe even in an android. A cyborg or something. They think it self-created a physical form to avoid destruction."

"How the hell are we supposed to find *that*?" he fumed. His head felt hot and his fingers numb.

Anjel looked sad. "I don't know. Our friends down there…they might…but I don't."

I should rip all these tubes out.

I should get Yeo's suit.

I should go back through the Door.

And waste every In city until they're all dead.

She saw him straining. She touched his arm and tried to push him down. Weak as he was, he sat up.

"Moz, stop it." She pushed harder.

"No, I have to—"

"Moz—"

"Damnit, Anjel. Go get Yeo. Go tell Frigg. I can't just sit here."

She looked him dead in the eyes. For a moment, he didn't care how beautiful she was. He didn't care about anything. He just wanted revenge.

And then Anjel flipped a switch on the machine beside his bed. Sedatives flooded his body. He fell into a sleep deeper than any he'd ever known.

* * *

When he crawled back to consciousness, he heard only fragments of what they said.

"…good as new."

"…for all that does us."

"…*Ins* are stepping up their game."

"…not even bothering with bots anymore."

"…the two new guys."

"…heard they didn't even last two jumps."

"…only a few suits left."

"…making more."

"He'll fight…"

"No he won't."

He opened his eyes. The room was hazy and lit with soft green lights. He knew he'd been under for a long time. His body felt better. But his head felt full of gruel.

"He's awake," he heard Anjel say.

"About damn time," someone blurted. It had to be Yeori.

He touched his chest, and felt his arms and legs. All the cables and IVs were gone; even the holes had healed. He flexed his massive arm, felt the muscle ripple, and knew he was whole again.

How long? A week? Two?

Doesn't matter. I'm back.

He sat up. He was lying on the bed in Anjel's room. Green lamps illumined her tiny apartment, and the tall, thin tapestries she'd painted hung from every wall. He'd seen her dragons, comets, and ethereal planets a thousand times, but here and now her paintings felt special. There were no artists like her, not on the Achilles, *not anywhere.*

Of all the people, she picked me.

Anjel, Yeo, and three scientists stood by the door. Their voices dropped to whispers when they saw him moving, which he hated. He clambered to his feet, and this time no one tried to stop him.

"Why so quiet?" He padded across the room. "Am I a ghost?"

Yeori shook his head in disgust. He'd known the old man to be in foul moods before, but the look Yeo gave his granddaughter was as bitter as he'd ever seen. With a grunt, Yeori stomped down the dark hallway beyond Anjel's door. The scientists, small and timid, shuffled after him.

Alone with Anjel.

Should feel better than it does.

"What's the matter with *him*?" he asked Anjel once the others were gone. "Damn near burned a hole right through us."

Anjel took his hand and led him inside. The door shut behind her, and she sank onto the bed.

"It's war, Moz."

"You mean—?"

She nodded. The lamps' green light mirrored her eyes. She wasn't crying. She didn't even look sad.

"Is Frigg going?" he asked.

She nodded again. "*Everyone's* going. Every man of age, even some of us women. Yeo said he wouldn't let *me* go, of course. I'd have argued it, but war's not in me. I've never seen an *In*. How could I kill one?"

It's easier than you think, he almost said.

"When does it begin?" he asked.

"Soon." She looked sick. "They've stopped making the Achilles' new grav-drive. They're just making suits and jump pads now. The first five will be done in a week."

"One for me?"

She stared hard at him. For once, her look reminded him of Yeori's.

"I don't want you to go, Moz."

"I don't want to either," he said. "But I *have* to."

"No you don't." She gazed at a tapestry of Jupiter. She'd painted it years ago, and it looked the same as the real thing. "You can stay here with me. We can work on the grav-drive. I've been studying. I can help them. And you can be our muscle. Move parts, carry gear up the lifts, do space-walks and installations."

He raised his brow. "A *worker*? You want me to lug things around the station while my brothers are out there dying?"

"No." Her voice sharpened. "I want you to *live*. We've done five jumps over the last two weeks. Want to know how many survived? Just *one*…just Yeori. Everything's different now. The *Ins* are onto us. They know where we're gonna be and when we're gonna be there."

"If that were true, they'd have smashed the Door already," he scoffed.

She shook her head. "Yeori said the same thing. The two of you, so hard-headed. You ever consider that maybe they don't want to smash the Door?

Maybe, just maybe, they know if they attack, the Kruberans will destroy it? And then what would happen? Think about it."

"They…well…they'd…" he stammered, "lose their chance to steal the Door's technology?"

"That's right." She almost looked proud of him.

He rubbed his eyes with his huge, meaty hands. He regarded himself: huge, strong, fast, and fully healed. The medics had fused every bone, decompressed every aneurysm, and sewn up every little wound.

"I'm good as new, they said," he murmured.

"Yeo wants you to fight." Anjel patted the bed, and he sat beside her. "I told him you've already done your part, but he didn't want to hear it. He thinks if we overwhelm the *Ins* with enough simultaneous jumps, we can beat them. It's stupid, I think. We don't even know where this *Out*-hating server really is. It's all just guesswork."

He put his arm around her. He could tell she wanted to shrug him off, but she didn't.

"Here's the thing." He squeezed her. "For every one of us that dies, tens of thousands of *Ins* are crushed. They'll run out of people, Anj. They'll have to beg for peace. Sooner or later."

She sighed. "No, Moz. You've got it backwards. We've got, what, a little over ten-thousand people on the Achilles? Maybe another thousand in the Krubera. And the *Ins* have got nine, maybe ten-billion. The math won't work. We can't kill them all. We can't even kill most of them without killing most of ourselves. Especially not if they've got some new weapon. And besides, all this killing...*we're* the bad guys now. *We're* the monsters. Don't you see it?"

"You really think that?" he said.

"I *know* it. I don't blame you, Moz. But we're the murderers. All of us."

He'd felt the same before, though he'd never admitted it. Nor allowed himself to think about it. Nor entertained the possibility that there might be some other way. He'd always believed the *Ins* were the enemy. *Our nemesis. Frigg told me so. Everyone told me so.*

Everyone except Anjel.

"If we don't fight them, they'll keep dreaming up new ways to get rid of us," he said after a long silence. "We'll just be sitting here, doing nothing in this damn ship. And then one day a missile will slip though. Or Jupiter will grab us. Or something will happen and the Achilles will pop. We'll be dead, and they'll keep right on dreaming. Forever."

She faced him. "What you're saying is; you're gonna fight? No matter what?"

"I'm not...I'm not saying that...I'm just—"

"...going through the Door." She finished his thought.

* * *

The next two weeks were harder for Moz than any other in his life. He stayed with Anjel, but she felt distant. He didn't know if she'd heard what he'd done in the Hatten. He was never quite sure whether she was angry at him for wanting to fight or sad that he might soon be dead. She never again tried to talk him out of it. Not when he trained in the gym for hours on end, nor when he went to watch the scientists weave the grav-fibers for the next set of suits. When he took trips to look at the Door, to marvel and wonder how such a thing were possible, she came with him, and she never said a disparaging word.

But in his heart he knew what she felt.

She's sad for me.

And angry, too.

She hates Yeo, Frigg, and all the rest.

And she loves them more than anything.

It's just like Yeo said: 'If Earth had only two people on it, two who lived on opposite sides, they'd still find a reason to kill each other.'

Ten days later, he woke in her bed to the green lamps and the tapestries, and he sat awake for a long, long while. He remembered the things he'd seen on Earth: *trees, clouds, and rain. Rocks, puddles, and sunshine. And the ocean beneath me while I jumped.*

He couldn't help but daydream. He longed to see Earth again. He wanted to be there while not at war, with no *Ins* or bots trying to kill him. He wanted to walk through the things called forests. He wanted to feel some other temperature than the permanent warm of Achilles. He wanted to taste the wind again. He'd only been there for a few hours, and yet Earth felt like the home he'd always wanted.

Anjel doesn't understand. She's never been. None of these people have ever gone there. If they had, they'd all want to fight. Not to kill the Ins. But just to live.

The Achilles isn't home.

It's a prison.

It's a box.

It's not natural.

It's not alive.

Not like Earth is.

I wonder what'd happen if the Ins came out of their towers.

Would they feel just like me? Would they want to live on Earth, instead of in a box?

They'd have to. Wouldn't they?

Anjel stirred. He kissed, caressed her, and made gentle love to her. She writhed beneath him, never saying anything, her soft gaze never once breaking from his.

Afterward, his body sang. His fears were forgotten, his desires for anything but Anjel lost in the aftermath of her touch.

"Moz?" She snuggled close.

"Yes."

"I have to tell you something. I'm afraid to say it. I don't want you to think I'm playing games with you."

"What do you mean?" He kissed her again. Her lily white fingers entwined with his rich, brown hands. She was so tiny, and yet she made him feel safe.

"I'm pregnant," she told him.

He supposed he should've been surprised. His heart jumped, his mind raced, but in the end the storm inside him calmed. Somehow, he'd known.

"How long?"

"Two months." She smiled. "Don't even know whether it's a boy or girl."

"You were worried," he said, "because you thought I'd be angry? That I'd think you were telling me so I wouldn't fight."

"Yes."

"Does Yeo know? Anyone else?"

"No. Just the medics. I can't tell the others. I only trust you."

He stood and paced the room. He believed her. *She didn't say it just to stop me from going.*

But even so.

"Moz?" She looked more vulnerable than ever. Oceans of love lived in her eyes.

"Yes?"

"There's one more thing."

"Don't tell me." He tried to be funny. "Twins?"

"No. It's Yeo. He's waiting for you."

"If he wants to talk to me, he knows where I am."

"No. You don't understand," she said. "He's waiting to talk to you *alone*. No me. No Frigg. Just you and him."

"Oh." His body sagged. "He's gonna ask. And he's gonna do it *his* way."

Anjel closed her eyes. "He won't ask you, Moz. He'll demand."

And I'll tell him to stick it, he thought.

I won't widow Anjel. Not now. Or ever.

116

Executioner

At dawn beneath a red sky, the jet hovered over Paris.

It was grandest of all the cities Rafe had seen. He stood in the jet's open door, the wind whipping his face as the jet hovered high above everything.

Towers everywhere.

Buildings between them. Broken and old.

The perfect trap.

Just as Absinthe had told him, the *Out* marauder had been drawn right in. Even now, Rafe could hear the thunderous footfalls, the buildings shuddering and streets cracking. When the jet dropped down to street level, he heard a distant tower fall. As the thing collapsed, it leveled a thousand-year old church. Chrome steel and ancient stone collapsed as one. The Champ de Mars, among the last green spaces in any Earth city, drowned in a sea of ash.

Rafe wasn't afraid.

He jumped out of the cabin and landed on a street. The blue-silver towers on the street's sides were narrow, but plenty tall enough to disguise his approach. Between some of them stood ancient stone structures, long preserved by *In* technology, yet utterly lifeless in repose. They looked like castles. Then again, he'd never seen a real castle, but only those dreamed by others in the ether.

The Out knows I'm here, he thought. *Couldn't have missed me coming.*

Five blocks down, a grey plume of ash opened its maw and swallowed several dozen buildings. Another tower had fallen. He knew it didn't matter. The server wasn't in any one of the lesser towers, nor in any of the monoliths encircling the legendary Spire of Eiffel.

The server wasn't in Paris at all.

He stalked down the street. He kept his fingers close to his wrist, poised to tap time to a stop. He walked by an ancient grey building. It looked so different from the perfect blue-silver towers that he stopped to admire it, but only for a breath. This was to be his final hunt. He just wanted it to be over.

He ran down the next block. His legs had grown stronger since leaving *In*. He felt faster than before. He swept past stained-glass windows on buildings older than the ether, and he glimpsed his reflection on towers that hadn't aged in centuries.

Time moved at its normal speed. He supposed he could've tapped the ebony band and strolled the last few blocks to reach the *Out*, but he hated the exhaustion that followed from using it too long. "Wait until you *need* to use it," Absinthe had told him. "It won't matter if a few more towers fall.

"We want the *Out* to kill *them* anyway."

He supposed he should've guessed it sooner. He should've known it when no one seemed concerned about how many had died. In each city he'd been to, tens of thousands of sleeping human beings had been snuffed in a matter of minutes by *Out* invaders and careless bot sentries. They had lain before him, burned and crushed, not one survivor among them.

Because Absinthe wanted it to happen.

Because some of the people in some of the towers don't agree with her.

He shook the thoughts out of his head. He told himself it wasn't his business if some of the dreaming masses feuded with others. Wars were inevitable, he believed. It didn't matter whether those who fought them were awake...*or asleep.*

The ones who speak against Absinthe haven't seen what the Outs can do.

Not that I wouldn't do the same if I were in their shoes.

He jogged, picking up speed. A fine glass mist rained over him. He crossed over an intersection pocked with *Out* footprints, and knew that when his enemy expelled his gravity, it'd shake Paris for a kilometer in every direction. He felt reckless, still not having slowed time. It didn't matter anymore. He felt as comfortable hunting *Outs* as he did doing anything in the real world.

Meaning he wasn't really comfortable at all.

He rounded a corner and caught a quick view of the *Out* man bursting out of a tower's side three blocks away. The giant chrome thing was one of few towers left standing in the Spire of Eiffel's shadow. When the first part of it hit the ruin of twenty other towers, Rafe stood steady in the ashen fields of the Champ de Mars. The earth shook. The world seemed ready to fall apart.

Another tower fallen.
Another ten-thousand dead.

As the ruined tower came crashing down, he tapped the ebony band six times and walked into the Champ de Mars. It had once been a grassy field, green and alive, but now the ashes were up to his ankles. The silence as he walked was pleasing. At his speed, sound was much too slow to catch him, and so he walked at peace, a lone vagabond swimming in a frozen sea of destruction.

When he reached the other side of the Champ de Mars, he double tapped the band and let the world catch up. The rush of noise, dust, and smoke washed over him. He didn't flinch. He didn't even feel nervous. He simply crouched behind a pile of rubble and closed his eyes until the thunder ended.

And then he heard the *Out* screaming.

"Where are you, you sonofabitch?" the marauder cried out. "That didn't kill you? A friggin shame! You got no balls? You some silver-bellied bot-lover? How about this?"

The *Out* gutted two more towers. They were smaller and closer to the Spire of Eiffel, but Rafe wasn't worried. He was far enough away that nothing the *Out* did could hurt him.

It's not a time-stopping trinket. He touched the ebony band.

More like an immortality bracelet.

Once the two towers finished dying and the cloud of ash thinned, the *Out* bellowed again.

"You still out there, bot-lover? We've got bugs on the Achilles thicker than you! What's that? You didn't *know*? That's right, dreamer. We bring a few back with us every time we kill a few thousand of you. Damn things crawl around my ass lookin' for a warm place to sleep!"

He'd never heard anything like this particular *Out*. The man had an accent different than any he'd dreamed possible. He sounded hoarse, angry, and old. He sounded barely human, like a man from a different planet entirely.

But then of course, I've only ever heard one accent ever.

In makes us sound all the same.

He peeked around the corner of a crumbling tower wall. In the red, dawnlit haze of smoke and raining glass, he saw the *Out* striding across the Champ de Mars. The marauder was headed for the Spire of Eiffel, among the last of the things standing in Paris' heart. The Spire was where Absinthe had arranged for the server ping to come from. It was the strongest ping she'd set up yet. 'Enough to make their sensors buzz so hard they'll hurt,' she'd said.

The *Out* roared again. *Would burst my ears if I were closer*, he thought. *Nothing's that loud in the ether.*

"Well, well!" the *Out* thundered. "What's this? A big ole' spindly tower! This place is famous, ain't it? Older than that time you fuckers shot us into space! It's coming down, bot-lover! Sit back and enjoy!"

He breathed hard for the first time since the jet had dropped him off.

I could save the Spire. Probably.

It's been there a thousand years. Absinthe said it's part of our history.

But if I kill the Out while his gravity's still up, it won't matter.

Nobody would be able to come here for decades.

He knew how the *Out* would do it. He watched his enemy walk directly beneath the Spire, roll his shoulders, and shout something, *a number*, out loud.

The shockwave of released gravity echoed out into Paris, shattering every building within two-hundred meters, vomiting gobs of dust and pieces of towers the *Out* had already broken.

Rafe covered his ears, ducked behind the tower ruin, and waited for three breaths. The shockwave washed over him. It hurt, but only a little. He was sure his bones shook inside him, and he half-believed the entire planet rippled.

But after three breaths, he stood and tapped the band eight times.

He walked casually through a storm of frozen dust and debris.

And he didn't stop until he stood a single meter from the *Out* marauder.

An old man, he observed. The *Out* still had his hands up with his palms to the sky, as if he were some sorcerer who'd just conjured up the world's end. His white beard moved ever so slowly, whipped by a wind Rafe couldn't feel. In the grav-suit, the old man looked powerful, as close to a god anyone outside of the ether had ever been.

But all his strength means nothing.
I hope he doesn't feel this.

Rafe drew out his knife. The short steel blade had nicks on it from the other *Outs* he'd killed. The grav-suits, even with their mass emptied and him moving at near light speeds, were still tough to cut.

He hated this part. Drawing a breath, he sawed the collar off the old man's matte black suit. Absinthe had always demanded he cut the *Outs* in three different places, but he'd never done it. He'd lied to her each time. One quick jab in the throat was all it had ever taken. People in the real world were soft, he'd learned. And besides, he didn't have a butcher's stomach.

He closed his eyes, braced himself, and delivered a short stab into the old man's neck. The steel suffered no resistance. It went in and came back out as if the *Out*'s flesh were air.

Don't look, Rafe reminded himself. *Never look.*

He walked away. The ruin of Paris stood still. Clouds of dust and dark ashes floated in the air. He brushed through the dead rain, and he didn't even wince when a sliver of hanging glass perforated his arm, nor when he dropped the knife on a street lined with frozen fires and pale corpses. He was supposed to retrieve the Out's jump pad, but he didn't care. He wanted nothing to do with it.

To hell with this place.

If this is reality, no wonder no one wants it.

The Spire of Eiffel collapsed behind him.

* * *

One day later, he sat in a medic bay in the highest floor of Alta Sur's tallest tower. His right forearm was bandaged and his fingers were numb. When the bay door slid open and Absinthe glided in, the medic bot fluttered away. Even *it* seemed to know when she was less than pleased.

"You're an idiot." She walked right up to him. The sterile white walls made her eyes look icier blue than ever.

"So you've told me," he grumbled.

She lifted his right arm, inspected it, and let it drop back down. He rubbed it as if expecting it to hurt, but felt nothing. The medic bot had juiced him up with anaesthetics.

"I called you that because it's *true*." She stood over his chair, judging him. "See, you pretty little boy, it just so happens if you walk through glass at thousands of kilometers per second, you get hurt. If this had been in your chest or your head, we'd be having a different conversation. It'd be one-sided. I'd be talking to your corpse."

He looked away from her. "I guess it doesn't matter. I'm done. That was the last *Out*, remember?"

She drifted away to a medi-panel on the far wall. The blips of his heartbeat leapt up on the monitor. He swore he saw her smile when she glimpsed his heart rate rising.

"Hardly the last *Out*," she said without looking at him. "There's a whole ship full of them. They're waiting for us. They're just a few million kilometers away."

He swallowed his fear. A cold stone in his throat, it hurt all the way into his gut.

"No. I dropped my knife. I'm not going to cut anyone else. I hate it."

She turned on her heels and faced him. Now she was smiling. It was as beautiful and sinister a thing he'd ever seen.

"Probably time for a new knife anyway," she said. "Considering how many you killed with the old one."

He would've gotten up out of his chair and stormed out of the room. But somehow he had the

feeling she'd hurt him if he did. *I'm bigger. I'm stronger*, he knew.

But she's crazier.

And I left the bracer in my room.

"I don't understand," he said.

"You don't *understand*?" she asked. "Or you're unwilling to admit you already know what has to happen?"

"I—"

She came to him. The way she walked was as rigid as ever. He felt dissected beneath her gaze, controlled with every flick of her long, narrow fingers.

She leaned close to him. She closed her eyes and inhaled his scent. He felt weak with desire for her. *God, she's perfect.* His thoughts were uncontrolled. *And she knows it.*

"Stop it." He looked away.

"Fine. Have it your way." She went to the monitor again. "You know you'll do anything I ask," she laughed. "*Everyone* does."

"No. Not this time."

She rolled her eyes. He wished he hadn't seen her do it. He wanted Toggle or Silk to be here. They'd always been sympathetic to him, even when he'd come back from the executions in a cold, cold sweat. He wondered where they were. He hadn't seen them in days.

"Rafe," she began, "Earth needs one more thing from you. Just one. And this time I mean it. You won't be chasing *Outs* in grav-suits anymore. You won't need to wander around any cities. It'll just be you and your little bracelet. It'll be easy. It'll only take a few seconds."

Only a few seconds.

She always says that.

"Stop *thinking*," she said. "And start doing. There aren't too many young men who'd shy from the chance to save the world."

He pushed himself halfway out of his soft, white chair. But then he stopped.

"I bet you counted on that," he snapped. "Me being caught up in some fantasy of being a hero."

She smirked, which always meant she was amused. "We're not stupid, Rafe. We knew someone as smart as you would have reservations. That you'd be conflicted. That your...*morals*...however muted by two decades in the ether, would show themselves."

He sank back into the chair and glanced at his heart-rate again. The blips quickened with his every breath. He felt hot under his skin, but cold in his chest.

What did Emperor call this feeling?

Fury.

"Always with the psychology." He gritted his teeth. "Why can't you just tell me the truth?"

"You want truth?" she asked.

"Yes. Always."

"Then ask."

"*Anything*?"

"Anything."

He looked at his hands, *as if they have the answer*. He peered up at Absinthe, *who's smiling just to make me feel small*.

"How do we always know where the *Outs* are? Every time. Sometimes it feels like I'm getting on the jet *before* the first tower falls."

"Satellites track them when they jump."

"So why not just blast them out of the sky?"

She let out a fake yawn. "They're moving too fast. Besides, I already told you; some of the towers we don't mind falling."

"So…" he reasoned, "if we're tracking them the whole time, then don't we know their point of origin? Where they're coming from?"

"Yes."

"And we haven't destroyed it. Why?"

"Destroy," she sighed. "Oh, you're adorable, Rafe. Why ever would we do that?"

"I don't know," he stammered. "Maybe…you know…to stop the *Outs* forever?"

"Oh yes," she laughed, "we'd stop them from coming in. For a while, maybe. But what about all the other ones? Up there, Rafe." She pointed skyward. "Their little ship is packed full of them. Probably nine or ten thousand after all these years. Blowing up the Door wouldn't stop them. They'd still be out there, learning, plotting…and breeding."

"The Door?"

Her gaze fell to the floor. For a half-breath, she looked almost vulnerable. But then the frost in her eyes returned, and with a glance she chilled him to his bones.

"It's the one piece of technology we haven't mastered yet. Carving up space with little holes. Turning a billion-kilometer flight into a three-step waltz. Yes, it's true; they've mastered gravity.

They've saved themselves from Jupiter's pull and built repulsors to stop our missiles. But it's the Door we want. Both to stop them from using it and to learn its secrets for ourselves."

"Why?"

She blinked at him. He could almost see the cold threads vibrating behind her eyes. "Imagine it…" She came to him and pressed her finger against his chest. "Doors to every galaxy, every system, every world. Entire planets turned into servers, powered by stars ten thousand times more massive than our own. So many of us think we've reached the limits of our imagination, that we can go no deeper into *In*. Wrong. We've barely scratched the surface. We're a speck of dust in a storm cloud. But we can be so much more. With Doors, we could harness everything *everywhere*."

"That's why you haven't bombed them," he breathed. "You don't want to destroy it."

"So smart," she mocked.

She sidled to the back of his chair. Not being able to see her unsettled him. He tried to stand up, but she snared his shoulders and pulled him back down.

I was wrong.

She's stronger than me.

"What do you want me to do?" He shivered.

"The jet will take you to Causcus. You've never been there before. It's ugly, rocky, and grey. You'll land at night, hike three kilometers south, and walk into the Krubera."

"What's that?"

She told him. About the caves, the sumps, and the impossibly deep mines the *Outs* had dug over the centuries, she laid it all out. She told him about the other *Ins* who'd wanted to invade and destroy the Krubera, and about her successful effort to deny them. The Door, it seemed, had been built on Earth *and* in deep space. It used splashes of technology stolen from *In* servers, but had been refined and perfected on the Achilles during the *Outs'* effort not to fall into Jupiter.

Absinthe desired the Door. She made it chillingly clear.

And the way she described it felt as though she'd been there since the beginning.

Like she's been hunting the Ins and seeking the Door for hundreds of years.

"You'll take the lift down into the caves." She severed his train of thought. "Don't worry; we have the code to enable it. We'll give you a map. You'll use it to slip all the way down to the bottom."

"Won't the *Outs* kill me? I mean…the lift won't work when I slow time. I'll be an easy target."

"Oh, they'll see you for certain." She smirked. "You'll just have to kill them. And you'll have to be quick about it. Can't let them self-destruct the Door."

He sagged. "Kill them? I told you; no more knives! I can't do it anymore."

She slithered to the front of his chair and leaned over him again. Her nose touched his, and her fingers closed over the tops of his forearms.

"If you like living, you'll do as I say," she whispered. "You'll show the *Outs* no mercy, else they'll make a puddle of meat out of your soft little skin. They'll open you up with grav-guns and hyperflechettes. And I'll be forced to remote detonate you before they steal your bracelet."

He paled beneath her.

She's not asking me to do this.

She's making me.

She pulled away. The clap of her shoes echoed against the floor. Before leaving, she glared over her shoulder at him.

"You'll go through the Door, Rafe. You'll turn your bracelet all the way up, and you'll worm your way into the Achilles' heart. You'll pop every airlock and decompress the entire ship. The *Outs* will end. It'll be the last conflict humanity ever faces. And you'll be the one to make it so. As the man who ended all wars, your name will ring eternal."

"What happens when I'm done?" he asked.

"Why, you'll walk back through the Door, of course. We'll whisk you right back here. I'll plug you *In* myself. By tomorrow night you'll be dreaming of your pretty planets. And you'll be free to long for *me* forever."

He didn't dare ask what would happen if he refused.

He watched her walk out the door, her perfect legs gleaming in the silver hallway lights.

And he hated himself for what he was about to do.

The Berlitz Exam

Anjel hadn't cried when she'd sent him out of her room.

She'd just stood by her bed, the green lights making ghosts of her eyes.

She hadn't said a word.

She hadn't wept.

Or frowned.

Or hugged him.

Or shouted.

Anything would've been better than silence.

"Moz?" the science officer said his name for the third time. The officer was one of few men aboard the Achilles taller than him, though the narrow man's shoulders were only half as wide.

"I'm ready," he grunted.

In the vast, empty room just beyond the Door Chamber, the officer stood behind him and sealed his grav-suit. The matte black fibers crackled as they came together along his shoulders. Some of the other men, *the whelps*, had complained about their suits' tightness. Moz had decided he liked the feeling.

"A second skin," he murmured.

"What's that?" The officer tugged the tiny thread on his neck, activating the suit's power source. "You say somethin', Moz?"

He shook his head. He had nothing else to offer. Thirty-three men had already gone through the Door ahead of him. He was upset to be the last. As one of only two veterans amongst all the men headed for war, he'd expected to go first.

But that honor had gone to Frigg.

"This suit's even better than the previous design." The officer patted his back and walked around him. "Faster reaction time, safer repulsors. The reload period after gravity expulsion is only three-point-two seconds. That's half what it used to be. Remember that. Might be useful in the field."

Fields are full of grass, not towers, he wanted to say. *Or at least they were in the pictures Anjel showed me.*

We're not going to fields. We're going to cities.
We're going to graveyards.

"Frigg already told me everything," he said. "A hundred times."

The officer, whose name Moz had already forgotten, backed away. "Yes…well…he asked me to remind you. Three seconds might mean the difference between life and death."

"It wasn't enough to save Yeo." He glared.

The officer stood aside and gestured to the silver-chrome plank leading to the Door. Moz sucked in a breath before walking. The last time he'd seen the Door, it'd been a black sphere, silent and still. But this time he saw dim lights glowing on its surface.

By now everyone else is getting ready to jump.
Anjel made me late.
Did it on purpose.

He rolled his shoulders, felt the suit stretch against his skin, and strode down the Door Chamber plank.

"You'll need to hurry if you're gonna jump with the rest," the officer shouted after him.

Thanks. He smirked as he walked.

Be glad it's me going instead of you.

Be glad you're not about to widow Anjel.

And abandon your child before it's even born.

He closed his eyes as he walked into the Door. Somehow he thought this time would be different, that the Door would sense his angst and turn him inside-out as he crossed hundreds of millions of kilometers in a few breaths' span. But the only thing he felt was Earth's lesser gravity and the cool touch of the Kruberan air.

He came through the other side. In the void of the cavern beyond the Door, three lamps shone with soft yellows. He scanned the deep shadow. He didn't see any of his fellow soldiers or any of the Kruberan people.

Not even Frigg.

Maybe they think I changed my mind.

Maybe I should have.

Leaving Anjel had been the hardest thing he'd ever done. In the days leading up to the assault on Earth, his heart had been set in stone. He'd meant to stay with her no matter what happened, no matter how the war had gone.

No matter how much they pressured me.

But Yeori had never made it back.

He'd never gotten the chance to stand up to the old man.

And when he'd found Anjel weeping in the dark for her grandfather, his heart had broken.

And his anger had boiled over.

"Don't go!" she'd begged. "Him being dead doesn't change anything!"

"How not?" he argued.

"He's just one man, Moz. There's nothing to avenge. He's killed what...a hundred-thousand *Ins*? What are you going to do? Slaughter a million? And *then* what?"

She hadn't understood. Yeo's death had changed everything. He'd needed to confront the old man, to tell him why he wasn't going to war, and that he wasn't a coward for wanting to stay on the Achilles and raise his child. He'd wanted Yeo to listen as he declared his love for Anjel once and for all. And he'd wanted the old man to watch as he made a life-bond with his granddaughter in the Achilles' chapel.

But the bastard went and died. Jumped at the chance to smash the Ins most powerful server. Did it even when Frigg ordered him not to.

Stupid.

Anjel's right. I'm stupid, too.

It felt strange that none of the Kruberan people were waiting for him. He supposed they'd escorted Frigg and the rest to their jump pads, but their absence made it too quiet. Anxious, he looked back to the Door, but it gave no answer. The Achilles' pale blue lights echoed on its surface. He shook his head at the spectacle. He'd expected it to wink closed after he came through.

Thought they'd close it behind us.

He started down the long corridor leading away from the Door. Pale lamps laid in the stone lit his way. The sumps surrounding the Door cavern had been grav-sealed centuries ago, but he swore he heard water dripping. The splashes sang in the vast darkness, the ghosts of water long ago evaporated.

Imagining things.

There's nothing down here.

He made it to the first lift. He hit the switch and heard gears grinding in the empty shaft overhead. Of all the technologies the Krubera had mastered, the lift wasn't one of them. It seemed to take forever, chugging down through the darkness, a relic meant to test his patience.

Finally it arrived. He was surprised to see no one aboard. A part of him was glad. Riding the old, creaking lift would give him a chance to prepare his mind for the fight to come. All this time, he'd brooded about leaving Anjel and being last through the Door. He hadn't thought about what he was going to do.

Or about the likelihood of dying.

He dwelled in silence the whole way up. The lift wasn't as slow as he supposed, and in moments it clanged to a stop. Another corridor awaited him. Graven through the stone by ancient Kruberan machines, the tunnel wormed into the darkness. More yellow lamps lit the way.

And still nobody's here.

He walked through the darkness, quickening as he moved. He felt agitated. His heart pumped fire through his arteries. The whole idea of sending so many of the Achilles' men through the Door was that they'd all jump at the exact same time. He hoped they were still waiting for him on the surface, that all the jump pads would be lined up and ready to go.

They'd better be.

If they jump without me...

He came to another lift. It was bigger than the rusted old thing leading down to the Door. The cavern opened up around it, but all the nearby workstations were vacant. Tools lay strewn on the ground. Pumps were turned off. A lone air generator hummed, but all else was silent.

Shaking his head, he pulled a lever and waited for the lift to fall. It came down in a quiet rush, reeking of oil. He pulled the gate open and flipped a switch. How the Kruberans dealt with so many lifts was a mystery to him.

Up. Down. Up. Down. They should've just come to the Achilles. We'd have squeezed them in.

The lift breezed him up through the darkness. Lights winked on as he rose, yellows, whites, and cold, cold blues. After a hundred breaths, the lift came to a silent stop. He stepped off, and the grandest of all the Krubera caves swelled before him. Centuries of machining had opened up the rock corridor to a hundred times its original diameter. Half the Achilles might've fit inside the voluminous tunnel.

Room enough for thousands.
Where is everyone?

He took ten steps into the void. When he'd first come here, he'd seen hundreds of people. They'd been zooming down the corridor in carts, climbing ladders to alcoves in the walls, and staring at him as he walked with the old woman on his way to invading The Hatten.

But now, nothing.

He peered up. A few folk were cowering in their alcoves. He saw the whites of their eyes glimmering in the lamplight. He saw them kneeling in their doorways, gazing down at him.

And then he saw the bodies.

He ran to the first one. It was a man lying face down on the damp cavern floor. A warm crimson pool spread beneath him. He'd only just died a few breaths ago.

He slunk to another pair of dead. Two meters from each other, a woman and a man lay crumpled behind a cart. The man had a steel pipe in his hand, while a grav-rifle lay beside the woman, humming with a fresh charge.

A fight? he guessed. *She didn't get a shot off. Someone opened her throat before she could do anything. Same for him.*

"One thousand!" he said while rising. His new suit made no noise as it swallowed up a thousand kilos of mass. At this weight, whoever...*or whatever*...had cut the Kruberans' throats wouldn't be able to hurt him.

"Two thousand," he said just to be sure.

He looked up to the alcoves again. He saw dozens...*no*...hundreds of people peering down at him. He understood. They weren't afraid of *him*. They feared something else.

He wanted to shout to them, but shivered the impulse away. Over his next ten breaths, he scanned the cavern floor. At least thirty more bodies laid in the gloom. Some had weapons, others didn't. All of them looked like they'd fallen without a struggle.

The Ins' new weapon, he feared. *But not down here.*

That's impossible.

As he counted the dead, he realized several were his brothers from the Achilles. He glimpsed Tyrin, the young man who'd been so eager during training he'd almost punched a hole in the ship. He saw Brunt, Kosi and Zamo's nephew, who'd signed up after Yeori had pressured him to avenge his uncles' deaths. They all looked asleep, lying in the shadows, swimming in shallow scarlet pools.

He spun to his left, then to his right. He expected flechettes, bullets, or bots with razor arms to swoop over him. He didn't know how the *Ins* had found the Krubera. He thought only two things:

Have to get back through the Door.

Have to close it before the Ins find it.

He backed into the gloom, and then halted. *This isn't right,* he shamed himself. *I can't run.*

I have to fight.

He jogged to a group of five bodies. All were men from the Achilles. Their eyes were rolled back and their throats opened up. He poked two of them in their chests. They felt soft.

Didn't grav-up.

Never saw what hit them.

Again he almost shouted to the people hiding in the alcoves. If anyone knew what had happened, it'd be them. But again he held his tongue. He rolled another body over. The man was the largest of them all, but had died the same way.

Frigg.

He swallowed hard.

Ghosts. He stood. *Fucking ghosts.*
I shouldn't have come.

Even with the yellow lamps in the floor and the cart-lights gleaming, he couldn't see much in the cavern gloom. One mass of bodies looked the same as another. The Achilles men had been marching in two groups, it appeared. If he didn't know better, he'd have thought they'd all died at the exact same time.

He stomped to the next group of fallen. Thirteen dead, ten from the Achilles and three Kruberans, lay silent against the stone. His footfalls made an awful noise as he stopped amongst them. A lamp cracked beneath his feet, and the dust floating through the failing light clung to the skin of his grav-suit.

"Where are you?" he shouted. "Come out and fight!"

He didn't care anymore. At two-thousand kilos, he had no hope of going unnoticed. Shouting or dead quiet, the ghost who had killed so many would hear him.

"What happened?" he boomed at the Kruberans hiding in the alcoves. "Where's the killer? I'll help you, but you have to tell me! Where's the ghost? *What* am I fighting?"

No one answered. No one dared. He lifted his arms to beseech them, but then caught movement near a cart whose motor still hummed. He erupted into motion, sprinted to the cart, and hurled it a hundred meters into the darkness. It crashed in a heap of metal, and then went silent.

A girl cowered beneath him.

He'd almost crushed her.

"Little one," he went to his knees and whispered, "what happened? I'm sorry I scared you. You have to help me. If it's the *Ins* and they get through the Door, my people are dead. If you don't tell me what you saw, *your* people are dead, too."

She was a pale little thing, white as Anjel and only half as tall. Her damp hair clung to her cheeks, and a glow-doll hung from her clutches.

"Where?" he asked her. "Just tell me where the ghost went."

With wide eyes, she looked up at him. He imagined he was as terrifying as anything, huge and dark and powerful.

"Where?" he asked again, this time softer.

She pointed over his shoulder. He looked and saw no ghost. Between him and whatever she pointed at lay dozens of dead. Beyond were only shadows.

"There?" he said. "Past the bodies?"

She nodded.

"I'm going now," he told her. "You hide, ok?"

"Ok," she whispered.

He rose and walked through the gloom. Tiny rocks crunched beneath his feet, and bloody footprints marked his passing. "Three-thousand," he uttered as he crossed the cavern.

"No."

"Four-thousand."

Got to be sure.

His footsteps boomed in the void. As he neared the cavern's far side, he looked back to the girl. He expected to see her skittering up a ladder, but she was right where he'd left her. He saw her nod again.

He knew the ghost was near.

140

He whirled. He thought he'd heard a cough, and he had. *There, in the shadows.* Sitting upright against the wall, leaning against a spike of ancient stone, a thin, pale man peered back at him.

The ghost, he thought.

An In, he knew.

The *In* was young, probably Anjel's age. He looked limp and bone-weary. His clothes were stark grey, his eyes sallow, and his right arm wet up to his elbow with blood. On his left wrist, a dark bracer gleamed. A tiny pip of blue light pulsed on the deadly-looking thing. Moz saw it and was afraid.

He rushed in and closed his huge hand around the *In*'s neck. He lifted the *In* into the air, all but strangling him. The *In* didn't resist, didn't struggle. He winced in pain, but said nothing.

"You did this?" Moz hissed. "You killed my brothers?"

Gasping for breath, feet a half-meter off the ground, the *In* couldn't answer. Moz lowered him to the ground, careful not to crush his windpipe. He needed to know before killing him.

"Did you do this?" Hate burned in his eyes. He pushed the *In* against the ancient stone, squeezing him just barely less than would kill him.

The *In* managed a nod.

"You killed them all?"

The *In* nodded again.

Moz almost crushed him. It would've been easy. At four-thousand kilos, he could've wadded the *In* up like paper. It probably wouldn't even have hurt.

"Why?" he boomed.

The *In* tried to talk, but sputtered.

"Why?" Moz lessened the pressure on his throat. "Tell me."

The *In*'s face paling, he gasped and fell to the cavern floor. Moz saw the blood on his forearm. *Maybe one of us got a hit in,* he hoped. *Maybe he's dying.*

Good.

He knelt. The *In* sat limp before him, barely conscious.

"Talk," Moz demanded. "Are there more of you? Why are you here? Tell me everything, and I'll make it quick."

"No...more." The *In*'s accent was like none Moz had ever heard. "Just...me."

"You're lying."

The *In* shook his head.

"Why are you here?"

The *In* peered up at him.

"Me?" said Moz.

"All of...you."

"You want us all dead?"

"No... *She* wants it. I'm just...the messenger."

"And they only sent one of you to do it?" Moz spat. "Arrogant."

"This..." the *In* pointed at the black bracer on his wrist.

"What is it?" Moz glared.

The *In* gulped down a mouthful of air. The bruises on his throat were already darkening. "It's...a weapon," he managed a whisper. "It's how...I killed...all the men...in the cities."

Moz felt his shoulders go slack and his fists fall open. That one single *In* could've butchered Yeo,

Kosi, Zamo, and all the rest hurt his heart. He felt fragile. *Like the Ins in their towers*, he realized. *Powerless.*

"One of you?" he exhaled. "Just *one*?"

"Just me." The *In* looked sick.

He considered ending the *In* just then. With a flick of his wrist, he could've slapped the life right out of him.

But he couldn't.

He's the same as I am.

Only I killed more.

I'm worse than him.

"What happens now?" he asked. "If I kill you, will they send more? How many weapons do they have?"

The *In* closed his eyes. Moz sensed the war raging in his mind. He'd felt the same when he'd invaded the Hatten, when he'd seen the bodies falling from the sky. He knew exactly what the *In* was thinking.

"They'll send more." The *In*'s voice was clearer. "One at a time, until it's done."

"Why just one?"

"She wants to control it. If she gives out too many of the weapons…rebellion. It's what she fears."

"*She*?" Moz made a face.

"Berlitz. She calls herself something else, but she's Berlitz. I should've…I should've known it sooner. She's an AI. An android. She's been alive for hundreds of years."

Moz shivered, but didn't know why.

"So we're all gonna die?" he said.

The *In* slumped against the wall. He didn't look hurt, but he wasn't moving like someone with murder on his mind. The light in his eyes was dim. Moz could hardly believe this was the man who'd killed all his brothers.

"The Door," the *In* murmured.

"You know about it?" said Moz.

"I was supposed to go through it. I would've used the weapon to cut all your life-support. You never would've known I was there."

"What the—?"

"But I don't want to." The *In* stared hard at him. "I'm not who she made me be. She killed the others...I know it. They didn't want this either. She took it too far. She let you kill thousands before she sent me. She knew where you were jumping. Maybe not today, but all the other times."

Moz's urge to kill the *In* evaporated. Now he just wanted to listen.

"What do we do?" he asked. "How do I stop her?"

The *In* cracked a slender smile. Moz couldn't tell whether he'd just had an idea...*or whether he's fucking crazy.*

"One of the jump pads," the *In* began, "it's set for Alta Sur."

"How'd you know that?"

The *In* ignored him. "Take the weapon."

"What?"

"Take it."

The *In* reached for his wrist. Moz considered cracking his skull open, but shivered the thought away. The *In* took the black bracer off and gave it to him. Moz held it in both his hands.

What the hell is this thing?

The *In* told him how it worked.

Moz sat there, listening like a child, as the *In* explained everything. He learned about how the bracer had been made, how it'd been conceived in the ether for one purpose and built in the real world for another. He learned about tapping the blue pip to slow time, the exhaustion that would result if he used it too long, and how to turn it off. Afterward, it all made sense. It'd taken the *In* just a few seconds to slaughter everyone. It had never been a fair fight. Nothing ever had. When he'd found his pale enemy lying against the wall, it hadn't been because the *In* was wounded. He'd stopped killing because he wanted to, because he'd made the choice to put his knife down, turn the bracer off, and walk away.

"The Alta Sur pad," said the *In*, "it's the one closest to the big boulder. You'll have to turn the bracer on as soon as you get to the top of the lift, else she'll detonate you. She'll know I'm dead and see you've got the bracer on. Your only chance is to fight the exhaustion and jump to Alta Sur without letting time catch up to you. Look for the tallest silver tower. You can't miss it. When you find it, knock it down. Level it. Kill everyone inside. If you see something beautiful fall from the sky, that's her. That's Sara."

"I—"

"And be careful," said the *In*. "Sara has a bracelet, too. She thinks I don't know, but I saw it."

"Who's Sara?" Moz felt stupid.

"Sara Berlitz. The *Out*-hater. The android we call Absinthe. She was human once. She was a famous psychologist. Kill her, and the war against the *Outs*…against *you*…might end."

It was too much, too fast. Bracer locked around his right wrist, he stood up and backed away from the *In*. He felt dizzy. He wanted to throw up.

"What's your name?" he asked.

"Rafe."

"I don't know if I believe any of this, Rafe."

"Doesn't matter. It's true."

"We should've never come through the Door. We should've stayed home."

"Wouldn't have mattered," said Rafe. "Sara wants you dead. She wants the Door. She wants the Achilles gone. If you don't stop her, she'll find a way."

"And you?" said Moz.

"I don't care. Not anymore. I don't want anything. I don't want them to jack me back *In*. I just want to sit here. I need sleep."

"So that's it." Moz looked at his huge, dark hands. "It's all on me."

The *In* closed his eyes. He looked tired, sad, and sympathetic. "Aren't you going to kill me now?" he asked.

"What?"

"I was sent here to end you, to go through the Door and destroy the Achilles. So…aren't you going to kill me?"

"No." Moz backed away.

"Never wanted to kill anyone."

Going Home

It never occurred to Rafe they might let him live.
He thought the huge man in the grav-suit
would've smashed him.

Or the ones hiding in the alcoves would venture
out and beat him to death.

Or maybe the little girl would pick up the grav-
rifle and scatter his bones across the cavern floor.

The first Kruberan to approach him was an old,
old woman. She had lines on her face a century deep
and eyes as blue as Absinthe's. She hobbled up to
him, knelt on the stone, and snared his chin in her
crabbed hand. When she spoke, he had to search his
mind for the language she used. It was different than
the huge man's. Her dialect was older, and had
evolved in a far different way than the *Outs* trapped
on the Achilles.

"He doesn't look like he's been sitting in a chair
his whole life," she said to him.

"I—"

"Tsk." She lightly slapped his face. "He shouldn't
talk."

He thought to argue, and then thought better. A
dozen more Kruberans wandered up behind the old
woman. Some were pale, others dark. Half were as
old as the woman, while two were children. He
recognized the little girl among them. She'd been the
one watching behind the cart when he'd murdered
dozens of soldiers and innocents. It must have taken

all of a second for him to kill them, and yet the way she looked at him was as if she'd seen everything at the same speed he had.

The Kruberans talked among themselves. He could've listened, but closed them out instead. If their choice was to execute him, he didn't care about the details. The *when* was more important than the *how*. And he assumed they'd be as quick to slaughter him as he'd done to their allies...*their family.*

It's what I deserve.

They took him out into the cavern. They weren't gentle, but nor did they hurt him. It didn't matter that no young men walked among them. He didn't dare fight back. Even when they walked near the still-pulsing grav-rifle, he never considered resisting.

"...only Mozelle remains," he heard them say.

"...won't be enough."

"...shouldn't have gone."

"...doesn't matter."

"...all be dead soon."

Away they shuffled him. They led him to blank space of cavern wall, murmured a password, and ushered him into the void that appeared when the wall slid open. For many breaths he walked blind in the darkness. He felt hands touching him, voices echoing on cold stone walls, and soft footsteps coming from every direction. At last, the voices fell away. He sensed he was alone with the old woman again. She took him by his wrist, tugged him to a stone slab, and slung a blanket over his shoulders.

"He will stay here," she said. "If our Mozelle returns, he will live. If our Mozelle never comes back, he may not."

She left him there. He heard a door clatter shut, more voices, and then silence. Once his eyes adjusted to the darkness, he blinked hard.

A room. Small and cold.

A stone bed. A blanket and pillow.

A Kruberan jail.

No one comes here much.

He'd been exhausted when Mozelle, the big man, had found him lying against the cavern wall. He'd used the bracer to kill everyone waiting on the surface for the *Outs'* mass jump. He'd knifed the two men who'd come up the lift. He'd shut the bracer off to ride the lift down, but reactivated it the moment it touched down in the grand Kruberan cavern. *Forty-two*, he'd killed. Some had been *Out* soldiers, others Kruberan guards, and a few had been unlucky observers. He remembered each one, for he'd counted them as he'd killed them. He remembered their faces.

And then, exhausted more by murder than by using the black bracer, he'd slunk away.

Now I'm not tired.

In the deep shadow, in a room lit only by a sickly blue lamp in the floor, he tried to remember everything that had led him here. He didn't blame Absinthe. She'd un-jacked him, manipulated him, and dangled the promise of her body if only he'd murder. But the deeds he'd done were his decision, he knew.

I could've stopped her.

Even if she had a bracer, she'd never have had time to activate it.

How did she manage to squeeze ten centuries of hate inside herself?

She's not even a 'she.' She's an 'it.'

I could've said, 'no.'

In his heart, he knew what had happened to Toggle, Silk, Trencher, and even Emperor. They'd all expressed doubts about what Absinthe...*Berlitz*...was doing. He remembered fragments of conversations with them, moments in which he'd been distracted by thoughts of Absinthe writhing beneath him. The others had hinted about how she'd gone too far, how the jets taking him to each city could've left sooner, how she let some servers be destroyed while protecting others.

Anyone who dreams out against her is expendable, he knew.

Those who don't care...those who sleep quietly...they're worth saving.

Toggle and all the rest are dead.

He remembered other things. He'd once glimpsed a laboratory in which more black bracers had been housed. He'd seen it, but hadn't understood until afterward. He knew what more bracers meant. If he died, Absinthe would use her masterful psychological skills to awaken and manipulate another. And another. Until all the *Outs* were dead.

She'd wake up a loner. A thinker. A weakling. Someone like me.

The Kruberans came to his prison door. One of them opened a hatch, slid something inside, and closed it. "Eat," the man barked, before marching away.

He couldn't help himself. He was starving. Absinthe hadn't given him a last meal before he'd left Alta Sur. He half-believed it was because she wanted him hungry, that she wanted him to hurry to destroy the Achilles in the hopes of returning. More likely, he imagined, it was because he wasn't meant to return at all.

She wanted me to destroy the Achilles and go down with it.

There'd be no one alive to remember the Outs.
No one but her.

Blanket over his shoulders, he ambled to the door and took his food. He expected a cup of crushed beetles, a platter of cavern-grown fungus, or a tin of stale, mineral-loaded water. It was none of these. The bowl was warm and filled to its brim with chunks of white vegetable, slivers of orange vegetable, and a deep brown broth. It wasn't like anything he'd ever eaten before.

It was delicious.

An underground farm, he knew. *They have one. Not quite the savagery she described.*

After eating, he sat on his stone bed. Being down here in a cold, dank hole felt like the opposite of *In*. In the ether he'd had permanent stimulation. He'd rarely talked to other *Ins*, but his planets had always kept him busy. He never remembered a moment as quiet as this. He didn't hurt. He didn't hunger. He couldn't see, hear, or smell. His absence of sensation was complete.

He admitted to himself he liked it.

For a long while he sat and thought and dreamed while awake. He closed his eyes and saw all the *In* cities in his mind. Vast and perfect, elegant and silent, they stretched to the ends of everything. This, he imagined, is what Earth would look like in a few thousand years.

Mozelle doesn't stand a chance. Sara will win.

In a thousand years, everywhere will have towers. In a few thousand more, a hundred more planets will be the same.

And no one will ever have to wake up.

He slept.

He didn't recall resting his head on the pillow or pulling the blanket over himself, but he slept all the same. Somehow his stone bed was more comfortable than his impossibly soft pallet in Alta Sur. Somehow he slept deeper than all the nights he'd lain with Absinthe.

He awoke.

More food had been put in his room. It was cold, but delicious all the same. He slurped up the stew, drained a cup of cold water, and plunked down on the floor. Toggle had tried to teach him about things he could do to pass time and ease boredom, but he couldn't recall any of the techniques.

What'd he call it? Exercise? Medi-tations?

It wasn't until a few hours passed he became restless. In the ether, there was no such thing as boredom. Every whim was satisfied immediately. Every moment promised change. But down here in the darkness, he wasn't built to cope. He'd never learned about patience. He liked the silence, but felt it closing in on him. He savored the chill in the air, yet shivered when it gnawed.

Mercifully, someone came to his door. He stood and walked to it. He didn't care whether the Kruberans were here to kill him.

Just don't send me back to Absinthe.

Don't jack me back in.

The door opened. The old woman, two young men, and the little girl stood before him. They said something in their strange dialect, and then led him from the room.

"He's not sick?" the old woman asked him as they walked down a long, narrow corridor.

"No. Not sick."

"He liked his food? His water?"

"Yes. He did." He caught himself talking like she did.

"Good," she muttered.

"Are you taking me to die?" he asked. He tried to match her accent, but was aware how clumsy he sounded.

The two young men looked at him with smirks. They were smaller than he was, but wiry strong. He saw their muscles taut beneath their pale shirts, and he knew they could kill him any time they wanted.

"Do you work hard down here?" he said. "Lifting rocks? Mining deeper?"

One of the young men laughed. The other opened a door and guided him through.

"He doesn't know our ways." The old woman walked beside him. "He's young and naïve. We don't mine anymore. We farm. We plan. We build."

"Build what?" He wanted to know.

"Things," she said. "Parts."

"What things?"

"If our Mozelle returns, we will tell. If not, we might never say."

He didn't understand. *What difference does it make?* he thought. *They don't know what I told him.*

They couldn't. And even if they did, why should it matter? I killed forty-two of them.

Forty-two.

It's only a matter of time before they return the favor.

They opened another door and led him into a great round room. He sensed he was well beneath the earth. He wondered if the Door was near, and whether or not he'd get to see it before they executed him.

In the round room lit by scores of soft blue lamps, they brought him to the center. Men, women, and children sat in a circle surrounding him. He counted two-hundred at a glance, but sensed more were sitting in the shadows behind the others. The two young men and the little girl left him, but the old woman remained at his side.

"Tell the truth." She smiled up at him. "We like the truth."

And so he did.

For hours, they asked questions. He wished Mozelle were here, if only to better translate his answers, as the huge *Out* had obviously understood him better. It didn't matter. The Kruberans, patient as the stars, sat in their circle and listened.

They asked him about *In*, about life inside the ether. He told them everything. They asked him about the technologies he knew, about the nature of his weapon, and about the other *Ins* he'd met. He answered without dissembling. He was surprised how they received his words. They showed no venom, no anger, no hatred. If not for the lone Kruberan guard with a grav-rifle slung over her shoulder, he'd have felt like an honored guest.

And then they asked how much he knew about the Door.

"Only a little," he explained. He'd told them the truth about everything else. He saw no reason to start lying now. "It's a wormhole, right? You've mastered gravity, like for your grav-suits, and you found a way to bend space with it. You've linked the Achilles and Earth. You probably send parts and supplies to the ship, but that's just my guess. Absin...I mean Berlitz didn't tell me much. I'm only guessing."

"Go on," said a Kruberan whose head was as bald as the cavern walls were smooth.

"I don't know." He looked at the floor. "I mean, maybe you're shipping parts to expand the Achilles. Or maybe you're fitting it with weapons...or defense systems. Or it's possible you've got more than just one Door. We figured out how you hacked our satellites to find our servers, but we never did guess how you stole so much of our science. Maybe you've got other Doors in other places. Do you?"

"No other Doors," said the bald man. "Just one. The science you speak of, it was your people who gave most of it to us. Not *all* of you want us dead."

"Oh." He felt stupid.

"And your device," asked another of the Kruberans. This one had an accent he found easier to understand. It sounded almost like he'd practiced. "How many are there? How many *Ins* will come to slaughter us?"

As many as Sara wants, he almost said.

"They'll send only one at a time until the Achilles is gone." He hung his head. "They'll capture the Door. And then they'll bomb this place to oblivion."

155

Even then, the Kruberans didn't look perturbed. They murmured amongst themselves for a time, afterward asking a final question.

"Do you have anything you'd like to say?" The bald man regarded him.

"Yes." He flushed scarlet. "I'm *sorry* for what I did. I know what you must think. I never wanted this. I'm sorry."

If they believed him, they never said. The two young men came for him, took his upper arms in their grasps, and hauled him back to his room. They talked the whole way, but he didn't listen. He found himself thinking of Mozelle, of his far-fetched hope the huge *Out* might somehow kill Sara Berlitz. The plan to give Mozelle the bracer had popped into his head at the very moment he thought the massive man would crush him.

But by now it's done.
The tower's either down.
Or Sara killed him.

He ate again. He didn't understand why he was so hungry. Or maybe it was that he had nothing else to do. After eating he shrouded himself in his blanket and gazed at the lonely blue lamp. His only thoughts were that he wished he could see the Door just once before dying, and how strange it felt he had no desire to go back to *In.*

He tried to sleep again. He tossed and turned on the stone slab. He didn't dream at all. The memories of his *In* planets, his grand schemes, and his desires to forever roam the ether had already begun to fade. Try though he did to dwell on the past and ride it into slumber, he lost it.

The world of the dreaming was dead to him.

Sara Berlitz had killed it.

Hours passed, maybe longer.

He sat, slept, paced, and ate. His room began to stink. His skin felt sticky. He thought he'd lost all sensation, but the longer he remained alone, the more he felt.

Shame.

Loneliness.

Boredom.

Restlessness.

Anxiety.

Calm.

He'd long known what the words had meant.

But only now did he learn what they felt like.

While taking a shallow nap, he heard his door open. Bleary, he looked up to see the two young Kruberan men. They came for him, and he concluded:

Finally going to kill me.

They led him down the hall. In his fragile state, their grasps on his arms hurt more than before.

"Someone wants to see you," one of them declared.

"You mean…before I die?"

They both laughed.

"Walk faster," said one. "Two nights in the dark, and you've already gone soft."

He did as they asked. He didn't really know what dignity was, but he tried to assume it. He stood taller as he walked, and winced none when they pushed him forward. He decided to ask no more questions.

All they would do is laugh.

They brought him to the sliding stone door. He knew where it led. *Out into the big cave.* He wondered if they'd cleaned up all the dead. *They're going to kill me in front of everyone.*

If I'd kept the bracer, I could've killed them all. Even the big one. Mozelle.

They said the password, and the wall opened. The grand Krubera cave wasn't brightly lit, but he'd spent so long in the gloom the lamps and glowing cart lights stung his eyes. He saw only shadows at first, hints of people watching him. The young men tugged him along and sat him down on the ground.

This is it. Don't scream.

What did Emperor say? 'Have some balls.'

"Rafe," he heard the old woman say. He didn't remember telling her his name. The Kruberans had never asked.

"Yes." He looked up to her. His eyes still hurt. She was just grey fog standing before him.

"Someone wants to see you," she said.

"I know. They told me. My executioner?"

"No."

He blinked and saw her drift away. And then a much bigger grey fog replaced her. He blinked again. He couldn't believe his eyes.

Mozelle was back.

"*You?*"

"Me." The big *Out* sat beside him.

"I should've known you'd be the one."

"No," Moz grunted. "I'm not here to kill you."

He looked the *Out* up and down. The big man still had his grav-suit on, but the black bracer was gone.

"You didn't go." He assumed. "You didn't jump."

"I went." Moz shook his head.

He felt his heart slow. "What happened? You made it to Alta Sur?"

"I made it."

"You found the tower? The big silver-blue one?"

"Yeah." Moz touched his chest. "We've got these sensors. Damn thing buzzed so hard I thought I'd been shot. Led me right to her. Seems she wasn't expecting me."

Rafe's hands were sweating. He touched his cheek, and his skin felt chilly. He didn't know what to call this feeling.

"What happened?"

"I remembered what you said." Mozelle smirked. "That I'd get tired from wearing the weapon too long. You were right. After the jump, I was gassed. Couldn't hardly walk five steps without wanting to sleep."

"And—"

"And...it didn't matter," Moz chuffed. "Wasn't gonna take a nap."

He shivered. He was sure he knew what the *Out* was about to say.

"You knocked the tower down. You killed them all."

"No." Moz shrugged.

"Wait—"

"Didn't kill anyone, not really," said Moz. "You told me she was a robot, and you were right. She must've sensed me. She came flying down the lift shaft, nimble as a bot. I knew it was her. She was pretty, just like you said she'd be. She'd have killed me, too. Had me dead where I was standing. But I'd tapped the bracer nine times. We were the same speed. Only difference was: I weighed seven-thousand kilos."

"Well?"

"She broke her knife on me, then her wrist. That's one realistic-looking bot, you know? Would've fooled me if you hadn't said anything. When her arm went flying off, I saw blue lights inside her skin. Reminded me of the hallway lights back home."

"You broke her?" Rafe's eyes had never been so wide. "Why didn't you just smash the whole tower? Why go in and risk it?"

"Because," said Moz, "I didn't want to kill anyone else. I'm done with death. I'll never kill again."

He hung his head. He'd had the exact same thought when he'd sat down in the cave.

After murdering forty-two.

"You'll never kill again," he said. "What about me? Won't I be the last one?"

"Nope," said Moz. "You get to *live*."

* * *

"It's over," Moz told him as they ate supper together in a private cave. A blue glow lamp shivered on the table between them. Hours after Moz's return, the Kruberans had arranged for the two of them to meet alone. Everyone seemed to understand the two of them had to talk.

Rafe picked at his food. It wasn't because it didn't taste good. Nothing had ever tasted better, in fact. It was just that he didn't expect to be alive. He didn't know what would happen next.

Where I'll live.

What I'll do.

Who I'll be.

"It's not over." He shook his head.

Moz gulped down another cup of water. "I get it. The *Ins* will still come for us. They'll find someone to replace your little girlfriend. Maybe it'll be worse than before."

"Not what I mean." He stared at the light.

"What, then?"

"I mean there's still billions of people living out their lives inside the ether. They'll never come out. Especially now that Absin—, I mean Berlitz, is gone."

Moz downed another three bites of stew. Rafe had never seen anyone as enormous, *or as hungry*.

"Nothing you can do about it," the big man said.

"*Do*," he repeated the word. He stared off into the nothing behind Moz. "I've never really *done* anything. I've dreamed and killed. Not much more. And now what?"

"Well…you've done *something*." Moz shrugged.

"I have?"

"You've helped end a war. As I hear it, it's been going on since before I was born. And I don't know when you were born, but I'm guessing it's older than you, too. And now it's done. Maybe. So that's something."

He closed his eyes. He remembered walking off the lift in the Krubera cave. He remembered the looks on the people's faces as he'd tapped his bracer. He remembered walking among them, a light-speed murderer, hating himself more with every kill.

He remembered knowing that one more *Out* would come up from the Door, a thirty-fourth after the thirty-three he'd already put an end to.

And he remembered deciding not to kill him.

"Why don't you hate me?" he asked. "Why didn't you kill me?"

Moz set his spoon in his empty bowl. The big man seemed hard-as-stone, but Rafe swore he saw *feeling* in his eyes.

"Wanted to," Moz admitted. "Thought about it when I found you, when I jumped."

"And?"

"I blame Anjel."

"Who?"

"Your Berlitz was pretty." Moz smiled. "I can see why you fell for her…for *it*. But there's no woman like my Anjel. You're alive because of her."

Rafe swore he saw tears in the *Out*'s eyes. Mozelle, giant amongst men, gave him a look he'd never seen before.

What's it called? Sad?

"See, Anjel said something a few days before I left," Moz continued. "She made a good point. She told me I was stupid, and she did the math for me. Since we…meaning me and Yeo and the rest…killed a few hundred thousand during our jumps, it can't ever be right. There's only barely ten-thousand people on the Achilles. Ten-thousand and one, if you count the baby Anjel and I are having. That means even though we dressed up like the good guys, we're not.

We never were. It wasn't ever about trying to get Earth back. It was about—"

"...revenge," said Rafe.

"Right," said Moz. "Revenge."

"What about Earth?"

Moz lowered his head. He looked sad again. "It's beautiful. It's perfect. But it's not home. I don't know the first thing about surviving here. No one really does anymore, not even these cave-people. The Achilles is home now. Out there, with Jupiter, with the moons, the blue lights, the stars...*that's* home. And even though I know it can't last forever, I still love it. It's where I want to be. It's where I belong."

Rafe looked at the table, the bowl, the stone ceiling, and the cold blue light. He never wanted to go back to *In*. He'd never fit in with the Kruberans. He realized he had no home.

"There are no *Outs*," he murmured. "There are no *Ins*."

"There's only people," said Moz.

* * *

Hours later, long after Moz had left, Rafe sat alone in a cold stone room. The Kruberans didn't bother keeping him in his cell anymore. They hadn't said anything, but he understood they meant to let him live. He was harmless, after all. Without his bracer, his powerlessness was palpable. Maybe they felt guilty for helping the *Outs* destroy so many cities, or maybe Moz's Anjel had gotten to them, too.

Either way, I'll never know.

He sat on his chair, eyes closed. The stone walls wept, which meant it was raining far above. He heard people moving, working, and talking. He envied them, for they had purpose.

They're alive. They're not In.

This is the real world. Everyone has a purpose.

Everyone but me.

He pitied himself, though he didn't really know it. It was another new emotion he'd never experienced, another sensation the ether hadn't bothered to teach him. He languished in it for longer than he knew, sitting in the dark, losing all track of the world.

It didn't matter that Absinthe was dead.

Not for me.

The war between cultures coming to an end was the best possible result.

But my part in it is over.

And then he heard footsteps behind him. They were heavy. He knew exactly who it was.

"Mozelle?"

The big man walked into the room with a green lamp swaying in his meaty hands. He wasn't alone. A woman more beautiful than Absinthe stood beside him, slender as a sunbeam, smiling a smile more genuine than anything he'd ever seen. She and Moz walked to him, and he sat up from his sorrows.

"Rafe?" said Anjel.

"Yes?"

"Is it true inside *In* you learn all about science?"

"I guess." He felt small sitting before her and Moz. "Me more than most."

"And is it true what you told the Kruberans? That you make planets? That you use real-world science?"

"Yes."

She looked at Moz, and Moz grinned.

"And it's true you don't hate us? You're glad to give up the war? You stopped even when you could've ended us all?"

"Well...yes." He felt ashamed.

"Good," she said, "we need you."

"For what?" He sat up.

"On the Achilles. We're leaving Jupiter, you see. We're never coming back. We're looking for a new home. We need your help."

"A new home?"

"Might take twenty years, might take a thousand," said Moz.

"We don't want to be *Outs* anymore." Anjel knelt before him. "And you don't want to be an *In*. Come with us. Come through the Door. I can't promise everyone will like you. They *won't*. But if you know science, and if you know how to remake planets into places we can live, they'll understand. You can say no, of course. You can stay here on Earth. But you'll never be able to leave Krubera."

"But if I do, the Door...it'll close forever?"

"That's right." She nodded. "Once we go through, it'll never open again. Most of the Kruberans will stay behind. They like it here, for whatever reason. We'll never make war with the *Ins* ever again. Even if they make a new Berlitz, we'll be long gone."

"Just think about—" Moz began.

"No." He stood. "I'll go. I want to live."

This is what I am meant to do.

About the Author

J Edward Neill writes dark fiction, sci-fi, horror, and philosophy – all for adult audiences. He lives in North Georgia, where the summers are volcanic and winters don't exist. He has an extensive sword collection, a deep love of wine and scotch, and a blind cat named Sticky.

He's really just a ghost.

He's only here to haunt the earth for few more decades.

Shamble after J Edward on his websites:

TesseraGuild.com

DownTheDarkPath.com

About the Artist

Amanda Makepeace has been drawing and thinking up imaginary worlds and characters since her childhood days in the suburbs of Maryland. Since those formative years, she's lived in the southern burbs, moved abroad to England, and now calls rural Georgia home. Her imagination is fed by a love of nature, myth and the fantastic. When she's not in the studio, you can often find her wandering the woods, collecting bones and other bits of nature for her ever growing natural history collection.

Amanda has done excellent cover work for J Edward's other novels, including Down the Dark Path, Nether Kingdom, The Sleepers, and Old Man of Tessera.

Her piece, *The Jupiter Event*, inspired the Achilles space-station in *A Door Never Dreamed Of.*

Learn more at *amandamakepeace.com*

 Téssera

Made in the USA
Charleston, SC
09 August 2016